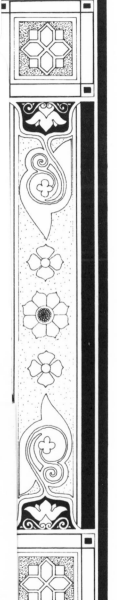

DO NOT REMOVE
CARDS FROM POCKET

DURANDAL

DURANDAL

by HAROLD LAMB

Illustrated by
Alicia Austin & George Barr

DONALD M. GRANT, PUBLISHER
WEST KINGSTON, RHODE ISLAND
1981

DURANDAL
by Harold Lamb

Copyright © 1926 by Harold Lamb
Copyright © 1981 by Frederick Lamb

Illustrations copyright © 1981
by Alicia Austin and George Barr

Printed in the United States of America
ISBN 0-937986-45-3

CONTENTS

                                                Page

Introduction, by Glenn Lord   13

Notes, by Harold Lamb   17

Durandal   27

ILLUSTRATIONS

Facing Page

Him Mavrozomes saluted profoundly, and his
boisterous companions were silent.
(See page 33.)   33

The Saracen horsemen engulfed the remnant
of the Franks. (See page 57.)   48

There was not a moment between sight and the
blow that flashed down. (See page 58.)   65

The *swish-swash* of something moving woke
Hugh of Taranto from feverish sleep.
(See page 72.)   80

Hugh confronted the foemen who had vanquished his followers a week ago.
(See page 125.)   129

No man, struck by that sword, rose again.
(See page 144.)   144

INTRODUCTION

by Glenn Lord

Of the scores of titles that graced the newstands during the heyday of the so-called "pulp" magazines, *Adventure* was unquestionably among the elite. It consistently presented fiction by the top writers in the field; fiction that was not only well written but usually authentic in background detail.

Harold Lamb and Talbot Mundy are perhaps the two authors most closely linked with the old *Adventure* of the era of the 1920s. Lamb was a masterful storyteller whose forte was the historical adventure, usually with an Oriental background. Lamb's knowledge of history is amply evidenced by the fact that he wrote several fine biographies: ALEXANDER OF MACEDON, CYRUS THE GREAT, GENGHIS KHAN, HANNIBAL, etc.

Inasmuch as Lamb's own comments on the background of DURANDAL are published herein, it would be redundant to comment thereon. Suffice it to say that this is a rousing tale of the Crusades, that lengthy drama of man's inhumanity to his fellow man. There are two other adventures concerning the sword Durandal: "Sea of Ravens" *(Adventure,* January 15, 1927) and "Rusu-dan" *(Adventure,* May 1, 1927). Doubleday assembled all three episodes in a slightly different version in one volume under the title DURANDAL.

Without a doubt Lamb's stories influenced many later writers, among them a high school student in the little Central Texas hamlet of Cross Plains named Robert Ervin Howard who would go on to carve out a career for himself in the pulps and whose works are enjoying an unprecedented vogue nowadays, forty years after his untimely death.

When Howard was fifteen he chanced to buy a copy of *Adventure.* As he later wrote: "After that I bought *Adventure* for many years, though at times it cramped my resources to pay the price. It came out three times a month, then."

Whether it was a coincidence or not, Howard was fifteen (1921) when he began writing. And many of his early efforts were Oriental adventures. Years later, in a letter to H. P. Lovecraft, Howard listed his favorite authors, among them, Harold Lamb.

It would be impossible at this point in time to say how much Lamb's fiction influenced the young Howard. Howard's keen interest in the East, his zest for writing historical adventures — almost all with a Crusades background — may have been from other influences. But the same somberness and headlong sweep of events pervades Howard's historicals that the reader will find in DURANDAL.

DURANDAL deals with the legend that the Arabs carried the sword of Roland to Asia, and it introduces Sir Hugh of Taranto and Donn Dera.

I want to say this about Sir Hugh. I've named him myself and drawn him from imagination, but also from life, because I followed the adventures of dozens like him. And the Sir Hughs of history were not confined to the crusades. They crop up all over Asia and were used to the personal and political advantages of shrewder brains. But after all the dust settled, and the annals and chronicles were written, the leaders who profited by his type we find usually as bare dates, and names and tombs. On the other hand the life stories of the Sir Hughs we've kept as part of our personal heritage — something that endures and belongs to us. Such men were Roland, the peer of Charlemagne, Tancred of the first crusade, Robert Longsword, and Count Robert of Paris (this last chronicled by Scott).

The legend that the Arabs took the sword of Roland

back with them to Africa and hence to Asia Minor, I have seen and read, but can not recall where or when. I've tried to find it again and know it is to be found, probably in one of the Arabic chronicles or Armenian histories.

A reading of *The Song of Roland* does not yield any mention of the sword Durandal after the death of the hero. It is just as reasonable to assume that the sword was taken by the Arabs (Moors) as that it remained lying under Roland's body until the Franks arrived on the battlefield a good many hours after.

As to the Franks, they were originally the people of Charlemagne who became known later as the French. Since the first crusade consisted mostly of French (Normans, etc.), the Muhammadans christened all western Europeans Franks, and this name sticks today. Go to the Levant today, or Mosul, and you will be a Frank.

Now the Roumis. In the first place the Arabs called Rome *Roumiah*. The Greek empire, being the nearer half of the former Roman dominion, was called by the Arabs the Roum empire, and the Greeks became Roumis. At that time they occupied most of Asia Minor, and when the Seljuk Turks conquered Anatolia, they fell heir to the name Roumis. But this was later than the time of the story.

The Antioch of the story was a city on the river Meander — not the Antioch of Palestine. This river, by the way, being very winding and casual in its course, gave rise to the word "meander."

Other words of the crusade era have come to have curious meanings today. When the old chronicler speaks of the *chivalry* of an army, he refers to the *chevaliers* or horsemen, who were usually nobles in the earliest days.

Accompanying and fighting besides the *chivalry* were the *sergens d'armes,* and *sergens a pied.* A story is told that Philip Augustus, a cautious monarch, formed the first body of the *sergens* to guard his person against the wiles of the Old Man of the Mountain. (The Master of the Assassins, a rather deadly sect of Muhammadans.) Although the *sergens* continued to be bodyguards for generations, they gradually became the mounted men-at-arms, carrying mace, bow and sword. Still later they could use lances. Anyway, that's where our word "sergeant" comes from.

At the heels of the "sergeants" in the medieval army we find the miscellaneous attendants and followers, called variously *Brigands, Ribalds,* etc. The *varlets (valerets)* or *pages* were the personal attendants of the nobles.

The custom of arming and equipping one or more men exactly like the real leader or king was common in medieval warfare. Often as many as half a dozen knights were made up like the king in order, as it were, to draw the fire of the enemy and safeguard the royal person. Usually they were badly mauled.

Now as to the eight hundred and the battle of the Meander, this all took place as related in the story. Eight hundred crusaders, who had joined the Greek emperor in the expedition against Kai-Kosru and his Seljuks, were killed to the last man.

There is, apparently, no trace of a survivor because the Greeks themselves reported the fate of the eight hundred, and the chronicle adds that the Count of Flanders was more wroth at the loss of eight hundred good men than pleased at the success of the Greeks.

The real happenings of the battle are vaguely related. It seems clear that the eight hundred Franks charged the Saracens before the Greeks came up; that they were surrounded and cut down to the last man, and that the Greeks themselves were then hemmed in by the Saracens.

The emperor was in command of the Franks as well as his own men. That these crusaders — the best unit in his army — should have been annihilated before his own forces were fully engaged, leaves the emperor open to more than a suspicion of cowardice or treachery.

Theodore Lascaris was subtle, persistent, daring and extremely clever. But he was not a coward.

Both Greek and Muhammadan chroniclers relate how Theodore Lascaris cut down the sultan Kai-Kosru with his own hand. Here is the Turkish account, as given by Petis de la Croix more than two hundred years ago: "Himself (Kai-Kosru) seeking the emperor in the mêlée, cries to his men to leave him thus duel. He meets the emperor soon, attacks him and casts him from his horse; Lascaris, half rising, pierces with his sword the horse of the sultan, and brings him down in his turn. He does not give the sultan time to recover, leaps upon him swiftly and cuts off his head. The Turks, hitherto victorious, take to flight" —

Although the Greek panegyrists and the Muhammadan annalist thus make Lascaris the victor over Kai-Kosru, another chronicler — Acropolita — says the sultan was overthrown and beheaded by an unknown hand.

Harold Lamb

DURANDAL

I

CHAPTER I

It hurts not the sword that its sheath
be worn, nor the hawk that its nest be
mean. — *Maqamat of Hariri.*

Mavrozomes pushed back the flap of his tent and
looked at the stars. Dawn was only three or four hours
off, and he had a task to finish before the first light.
Always, before a battle, Mavrozomes had this task.

He took up the insignia of his office, which was
armorer to the Emperor Theodore. The silver hammer
he thrust into his belt and the white leather glove
likewise. Mavrozomes was a creature of habit, and
though he did not like to think, it was now necessary for
him to do so.

Through the mist of the ravine he watched the red
eyes of light that were the fires of the men-at-arms, and
he sighed. Ten thousand men lay or sat by their weapons
in this ravine, and from the ten thousand he must select
one. This was his task and it troubled him.

He had put off doing it until he heard the advance
division getting their horses out of the lines, stumbling

27

about in the mist and talking low-voiced. If the advance was mounting to move forward, there would surely be a battle, because Sultan Kai-Kosru lay yonder in the plain, beyond the ravine, with a good many more than ten thousand paynims.

In his own mind Mavrozomes was not quite clear as to whether the paynims were Turks or Arabs;* but he knew very well they were Muhammadans — bearded gentlemen who wielded curved swords that had keen edges.

Somewhere in the plain was a small river, called the Meander, and on the river a walled town. The town was Antioch and belonged to Sultan Kai-Kosru, and this town the crusaders meant to take for themselves before the sun had set again. Mavrozomes wished that the paynims were not so numerous — or that the Emperor Theodore had decided not to give them battle.

There was little chance of the helm or hauberk of the Emperor Theodore suffering harm on the morrow — so the armorer reflected. His work had been to polish, not to mend, his master's chain mail.

Theodore Lascaris, the gracious, the all-governing, the lord of Constantinople and Nicea, would not be within reach of sword edge or arrow tip on the morrow. But the paynims would seek him, and for this reason —

---

*Kai-Kosru was sultan of the powerful Seljuk Turks and Turk-omans in the early thirteenth century.

and to hearten the emperor's men — someone else must wear the gold inlaid armor of Theodore, the surcoat with the royal purple border, and the shining helm surmounted by the griffon crest.

Behind the bars of the steel casque the face of this unknown would not be seen. The foeman would notice him, would seek him out and perhaps slay him. But the person of the real Emperor Theodore would be safeguarded.

It was not a simple matter to select this make-believe monarch. The man would need to be a weapon wielder of skill and daring, to keep safe the imperial standard that would follow him through the course of the battle. He must be a man of clear mind and tight lip, and one who could hold up hand and head in chaos. Certainly many of the crusaders would believe that he was actually the Emperor Theodore.

Since the odds were he would not live to see the sun set, he must needs be a man of courage.

So Mavrozomes reasoned, and made his way past the snoring and growling ribalds who tended the fires and horses and stole what they might. He avoided the groups of sergeants-at-arms. The mock emperor should be of gentle blood.

He circled around the pavilions of the nobles, before which motionless banners drooped. Once a lantern was swung close to his face and he waited until the patrol had clanked and stumbled away from the mist. He waited because, in the gleam of light, he had seen a man sitting on a stone.

Mavrozomes had never before seen a man just like this one, who sat alone in the mist. A long staff, iron-bound, lay across his bare knees, and his long, loose-jointed arms rested upon the staff. He wore a short, sleeveless shirt of clumsy plate mail. Over this a cloak was thrown carelessly, and the cloak was white with a gold clasp at the throat and a hood upon the shoulders.

"What man are you?" asked the armorer.

It was clear to him that this stranger did not wear a knight's belt, and the only weapon hanging from his leather girdle was a short falchion with a horn handle, little larger than a knife.

The stranger did not look up.

"I am Donn Dera."

Soft as a woman's was his low voice. But his face was dark and bony, the hair shaggy over eyes and forehead — shaggy and fiery red.

"What lord do you follow?" demanded Mavro-zomes, who was plagued by a demon of curiosity. "What do you here?"

By the voice of the stranger, he was neither Greek nor Italian, Fleming nor Frenchman. His hairy, withe-bound legs were like a ribald's or a thrall's, and he certainly had no helmet about him anywhere. Nor upon his cloak was there any sign of the cross worn by every follower of the Emperor Theodore.

"I wreak destruction. Yea, I look for rapine."

Mavrozomes stepped back a pace, but the man in the cloak appeared to take no heed of him. About the stranger was something sad and lonesome, and un-yielding. Thralls did not speak to the armorer of the emperor like that.

"Are you noble-born, Donn Dera?" asked Mavro-zomes. For a space the stranger made no reply.

Then he pointed toward the faint glow where the stars were failing.

"Yea," he said gruffly, as if giving tongue to the burden of his thoughts, "the day comes and there will be a rare feeding of ravens, and whetting of sword edges — there will be sorrow and blood that the wolves will drink. I have no more words for you, little man."

Reminded of his mission and the passing of time, Mavrozomes stifled curiosity and hurried on. Glancing over his shoulder he saw that Donn Dera was still sitting on his stone, alone in the chilling mist.

Mavrozomes picked his way through the tents and the sleeping groups to the fires of the Franks.

These Franks, following their custom, had settled themselves at a little distance from the warriors of the Emperor Theodore. Eight hundred of them, from France and Norman England and Flanders had joined the master of Constantinople in his march against the Saracens. They were the flower of his fighting men — long-limbed and high-tempered — utterly reckless of themselves or others.

He asked his way, and so came to a fire where a dozen men roared over wine cup and dice board. They greeted him with an instant silence, and then quick outcry.

"Ho, the pagan gods have sent a messenger! Here is Thor with his hammer."

"Nay — Saint Denis! — only mark the gauntlet. He has been flying pigeons!"

A dark-browed Provençal — a minstrel, by token of the gittern resting upon one knee — smiled and swept skilled fingers across the strings.

"Messers," cried he, "attend ye!" And he pitched his fine voice to a ringing couplet:

"His hair is oiled — painted his cheeks.
A paladin he — of the Greeks!"

"Well and truly sung, Marcabrun!" declared a giant Frank solemnly, when the roar of mirth had subsided. "You have put heart into yon baron of Constantinople. I trow he'll make a brave stand in the camp when we fare forth to smite the Saracens."

In truth, blood had darkened the smooth cheeks of Mavrozomes. The Franks held the fighting qualities of

Am Mavronomes saluted profoundly,
and his boisterous companions were silent.

the Greeks in as much contempt as the men of Constantinople held the savage manners of the crusaders from the west, whom they called barbarians.

"Enough!" cried a young knight suddenly. "Se ye not, messers, this armorer bears the insignia of his office?"

The speaker was a youth who had grown to the full strength of manhood. He had put aside his mail and knelt by the fire in stained and creased chamois leather, scarred and rent in more than one place. Broad, black leather strengthened by silver plates belted him above slender hips. His long body upbore the chest and wide shoulders of a man accustomed to the weight of armor.

Wide and firm-set were his lips, and friendly his gray eyes. There was in him more than abundant physical vitality — the eagerness and wilfulness of a boy who has never known shame or suffering. This beauty of head and bearing — or the peculiarity of his long, red-gold hair — had bestowed upon him the nickname of Hugh the Fair. Him Mavrozomes saluted profoundly, and his boisterous companions were silent.

"To Sir Hugh of Taranto, called the Fair peer of Christendom, most puissant of the knights of the Cross, descendant by direct line of Charlemagne the Great" — he began.

"Enough!" cried the youth again, ill-pleased. "What will ye, Messer Armorer!"

Mavrozomes drew the white gauntlet from his

girdle, arousing the instant expectancy of the Franks. Although he knew well that these barbarians from over the sea were not at all patient, he did not know how to curtail his ceremonious message.

"*Equites illustrati,*" he announced, "noble knights, Mavrozomes, *armiger imperatoris,* gives greeting and a summons to Sir Hugh from the most illustrious, most gracious emperor — " he lifted the light silvered basinet from his head, and the giant Frank sniffed loudly, aware of musk and oil — "Theodore Lascaris" — he bent his head, throwing up his left hand before his eyes as if dazzled by the very mention of the imperial name — "in this wise. To Sir Hugh hath fallen the honor above price and claim, the distinction of bearing upon his person the imperial and shining helm, the emblazoned shield of the Comneni, so that in the battle with the Saracens of Kai-Kosru, the great sultan, he shall worthily uphold the name and honor of the emperor, strike fear into his foes, and by so doing safeguard the person of Theodore. I await, Sir Hugh, your answer to the summons."

The eyes of the youth kindled and he struck palm to the massive pommel of the sword at his side.

"It likes me well, Messer Mavrozomes!"

The Greek bowed.

"Thus, the charge is accepted. The imperial standard will accompany you. And it would be advisable," he added thoughtfully, "to choose certain of your brother knights renowned by name and deeds, to act as body-guard. Of a truth, the Saracens will not deal lightly with you and your fellows, my Lord."

He could have said nothing better suited to the mood of the men. The minstrel cried that he would ride with Sir Hugh. Only the bearded stalwart, the knight who had baited Mavrozomes, frowned blackly, and stood up, folding his arms on his chest.

"It likes me ill, Greek. I have fought ere now with sword and lance and mace against the Saracens. And I wit well that they will make a set upon Sir Hugh. Hath not your emperor men of valor to his command that he summons a boy such as this to a passage perilous?"

To this Marcabrun took exception.

"Ill said, Rinaldo! Were the emperor to give this honor to a Greek, it would be an affront upon us."

"Now out upon thee, Marcabrun," retorted Rinaldo, "with thy qualms and punctilios! If affront it be, to choose a Greek for the mock-emperor, I say this — when the battle is at an end, we will go over to the Greeks and wipe out the affront with our swords."

"Hast forgotten, Rinaldo," quoth the minstrel, "that we have sworn fellowship with the Greeks and service to the emperor?"

"Well, we did not swear we would not draw blade upon them." And the bearded Rinaldo glared at Mavrozomes. "I have said it likes me ill, and what I say I will maintain with hand and glove. Full well the cowardly Greeks know that this adventure will give Hugh's flesh to the wolves and ravens."

"Too much have you said, unwisely, Rinaldo," cried Hugh. "Theodore is our leader in this venture and his men are our brothers-in-arms. It is their thought to do honor to the Franks."

"If ever a Greek thought of aught but his own skin and wallet," quoth Rinaldo stubbornly, "then am I a cup-shot churl."

"Messers," spoke up a man who had been silent hitherto — a gray-chinned Norman, blind in one eye — "it is true that among the Crosses there is no baron the equal of Sir Hugh. His valor and prowess at arms is proven. Methinks the honor would be greater did this Theodore yield to him the baton and horn of leadership in this battle. Right willingly would all the Christian knights follow Hugh in that case."

"Aye," shouted Rinaldo, "let it be so! The Greeks shall give the command to Hugh."

Mavrozomes raised his hands in horror, as if he had witnessed sacrilege.

"O ye peers of Christendom!" laughed the minstrel. "Are ye querulous churls, or men of faith? Theodore is crafty and wise in leadership. Have ye followed him a hundred leagues into Asia, to bay at him now, like dogs?"

"Wherever your folly leads you, Marcabrun," declared the morose Norman, "my step shall go as far as yours. But Theodore is a fox with an eye to his burrow. If it suited him, he would betray us."

"To whom?" exclaimed the minstrel. "To the jackals and kites? To the Saracens, who hate him in greater measure than they fear us?"

Hereupon Hugh picked up his leatherbound sword, and lifted his hand.

"An end of words! We must bear ourselves so that no foeman comes anear the person of the true Emperor, and this we shall do right willingly."

"Aye so," muttered Rinaldo, "we shall so bear us, by God's grace. And before we mount into the saddle, Theodore shall have proof of our will."

And when Hugh had departed with Mavrozomes, Rinaldo summoned to him the men who had gathered around the fire, hearing rumor of the choice that had fallen upon the young knight. To them the big Frank spoke earnestly, low-voiced, and there was no more roaring of songs or clinking of cups.

In the tent of the armorer, Marcabrun, the Provençal, fingered his guitar in high good humor. Marcabrun was already armed, and he followed with experienced eye the fingers of Mavrozomes, who had slipped over the stalwart body of Hugh a double chain mail threaded with gold inlay. From foot to throat the young knight was clad in the glistening mesh. Mavrozomes buckled on him the wide sword belt of the knight, and laced to the steel collar of the hauberk the unmistakable helm of the Emperor Theodore.

It pleased the minstrel that this casque should be inlaid with gold, and surmounted by a cleverly fashioned griffon with flaming rubies for eyes. The two cheek plates and the long nasal piece hid Hugh's features except for eyes and chin. But Marcabrun did not think the shining helm would ward as stout a blow as his own plain conical steel cap.

When the long triangular shield, emblazoned with the Greek cross on a purple field, was slung about the youth's neck, the minstrel gave voice to his delight.

"Olá, messers!" he cried. "It were well that this hour should be rendered joyous with a fitting lay."

"What were better," ventured the armorer courteously, "than the illustrious song of the Franks, of the hero Roland and his sword?"

A shadow crossed the minstrel's brow.

"God forfend! Roland, the peer of Charlemagne, came to death by treachery in a day agone — aye, and the chivalrous Olivier, his brother-in-arms."

"There is no song like Roland's," said Hugh calmly. "I know it well. Sing, O Marcabrun, for this is a joyous hour."

For a moment the minstrel scanned his friend, thinking that the erect form of the youth made a finer figure in the imperial armor than the lean and stooped Theodore. Smiling, he struck the strings under his hand, and the Greeks fell silent to listen.

"It is the prelude of the great battle that I say and relate," he chanted. "Give heed O noblemen and lieges, to the words of Roland, in the vale of Roncevalles, on the day that Charlemagne passed with his peers through the Pyrenees, and the two heroes held safe the rear of his host —

> "Olivier climbed to a mountain height,
> Glanced through the valley that lay to right;
> He saw advancing the Saracen men,
> And thus to Roland he spake again —
> 'I have seen the paynim,' said Olivier.
> 'Never on earth did such host appear;
> A hundred thousand, with targets bright,
> With helmets laced and hauberks white,
> Erect and shining their lances tall;
> Such battle as waits you did ne'er befall.
> In mighty strength are the heathen crew,'
> Olivier said, 'and our Franks be few;
> My comrade, Roland, sound on your horn;
> Charles will hear, and his host return.'

" 'I were mad,' said Roland, 'to do such deed;
Lost in France were my glory's meed.
My Durandal shall smite full hard,
And her hilt be red to the golden guard.
The heathen foemen shall find their fate,
Their death, I swear, in the pass they wait — ' "

A swift roar of voices interrupted the measured tones of the minstrel, and a thudding of hoofs and grating of steel was heard without the tent. Rinaldo thrust in his head, coifed and helmeted.

"Well and truly sung, Marcabrun. The Crosses have sent hither a body guard, and await sight of Hugh. Come!"

Going from the tent with the young knight, Marcabrun saw that a gray light overhung the dark ravine, and in the mist he made out a forest of spears. A close array of mounted men surrounded them, and Hugh's battle horse was held in readiness before them. All the eight hundred crusaders had assembled to accompany Hugh, instead of the small band suggested by Mavrozomes.

The knight in the imperial armor halted as if struck when he beheld them, and Rinaldo laughed under his breath.

"Lo, sir brother, here is thy body guard, and if this day thou art slain, full eight hundred bold men will bear thee company."

Sir Hugh looked silently upon the restless war

horses, the rows of grim-faced warriors. He went to his charger, picked up the curved horn that hung from its chain at the saddle peak and sounded a blast that echoed from rock to rock in the ravine — a rallying note that the archers who had gone forward in the first advance heard and understood.

But Mavrozomes slipped from his tent and ran, a shadow moving through the mist, to where a light Arab courser had been saddled and kept waiting in readiness. Mounting hastily, he trotted through the encampment of the Greeks, where nobles and servants were coming forth to learn the meaning of the Franks' trumpet call.

Where a wall of cloth had been stretched across the ravine he dismounted and approached two spearmen in silvered mail, who lifted their weapons as he gave the password. At the entrance of a silk pavilion he was scrutinized sharply by the guards and recognized. Taking on one arm his basinet, he raised high his right arm and empty hand, and, bending forward at the waist, crept as a jackal crawls into the presence of Theodore Lascaris, the emperor.

When he beheld under his feet a long, narrow carpet, he bent still lower and drew his right arm across his eyes. Sidewise, he peered at the gilded sandals, the long cloth hose of Greek attendants, until he judged it was time to speak. There had been a deep silence in the pavilion.

"Is it permitted, O Greatest of the Comneni, to

speak and live? The servant of thine Illustriousness hath gained the consent of the most renowned of the Franks, who now goes forth in thine armor — "

"What was the trumpet call?"

A quick, modulated voice asked the question.

"May it please your Grandeur, that was the rallying note, to announce the advance of the Crosses. From horse sergeant to baron, they ride forth, led by the champion who is garbed for the day in thy royal semblance — may thy years be increased, and never foe come anigh thee!

"To them likewise I gave thine order, that they should pass from the ravine and attack, and that thy host would follow — "

Mavrozomes paused, to discover if his master wished him to proceed, and again he took account of legs to make certain that no hostile ear should hear what next he said.

"It has happened in all things as thou hast desired it. Lo, the Franks go against the sultan and his array. The Saracens will be confounded by the onset of the barbarians. There will be a slaughter, and a ceaseless play of weapons. When the day is near its end, then may the invincible host of the emperor advance to victory."

"Aye," said the reflective voice, "it is well done. And yet — will not the Franks turn back when they find they are not supported by my companies?"

"Turn back they will not. They are like unleashed

hunting hounds at scent of a stag. Their champion may be smitten down, their standards reft from them, and still they that breathe will fight on. It is the nature of the barbarian."

Another voice was heard, modulated and unctuous as a flute attuned to the ear of a musician:

"May I, the Caesar* of your grandeur, speak and live? When the imperial host advances upon the broken Saracens, a remnant of the barbarians may yet stand in arms. *Imperator Maximus,* it were well that *none* should outlive this day."

"Aye, great Lord," put in Mavrozomes eagerly, "the barbarians have blunt tongues and scurrilous. Not an hour agone they did blaspheme thy Majesty — "

---

*Caesar — The Greek Empire was the last fragment of Roman dominion, comprising, in the early thirteenth century, what is now the Balkans, Greece, the eastern islands of the Mediterranean, and Asia Minor, along the coast of the Black Sea, and as far to the south as Palestine. Constantinople was its imperial city.

It had been ruled for centuries by the family of the Comneni. Now the warlike Seljuk Turks had settled themselves in the heart of Asia Minor, and the crusaders — exasperated beyond endurance by the double-dealing of the Greeks — had driven the emperor out of Constantinople, into Asia. The policy of Theodore was to weaken the crusaders while pretending to be their friend, and to break up the Seljuk power.

The title of Caesar was the second highest in the empire, and was given in theory to the commander of the imperial host — in reality it was sold to money lenders, even Tatars, and to several at the same time.

"Thy mission is accomplished, Mavrozomes," the cryptic voice of the emperor broke in. "Take care to guard thy tongue!"

Not once had the armorer looked up into the lean and pallid face of Theodore Lascaris. He did not see the tawny eyes pucker thoughtfully, or the down-curving lips tighten. Yet he heard the unmistakable clink of gold coins.

Theodore, weighing within his fingers a small purse that lay in an ivory casket at his side, was considering how greatly he need reward the armorer. And Mavrozomes, from the corners of his eyes, was watching the hand of the emperor.

II

CHAPTER II

THE FRANKS

When the sun was high, the last files of the crusaders
emerged from the ravine and formed on the sandy
plain. Close at hand upon the left, the river Meander
wound through dense rushes where waterfowl clamored
and swooped. The ground in front sloped gently down
to a dry bed of a stream, and ascended gradually to a line
of hillocks a quarter mile away.

On this ridge the host of Kai-Kosru awaited them.

The Saracens seemed to be drawn up in no par-
ticular formation. Groups of horsemen were visible
moving through the gullies between the hillocks, and
the heights were held in strength. Far to the right,
clusters of mounted archers trotted out and turned back
again.

This continual motion of the Saracens and the heat
haze that clung to the valley bed concealed the true
numbers of the sultan, and the little group of leaders

that surveyed the field from in advance of the crusaders' ranks watched it all in silence.

"I like it not," quoth the gray Norman, brushing the sweat from his eyes.

"What is their strength?" wondered Marcabrun, who had put aside his gittern, and was drawing taut the lacing of his coif.

"Three — five times our own," answered Rinaldo impatiently. "Come, messers, let us advance out of this hell-hole and try them with sword strokes."

"More lie hidden beyond the upland," insisted the Norman, "and it seems to me that here we have the full power of Seljuk and Turkoman under the banner of Kai-Kosru."

"Let it be so!" cried Rinaldo. "We may not now draw back. If, indeed, twenty thousand paynim lurk on yonder height, we should do ill to abide their charge. Forward, say I."

"Aye!" acclaimed the impetuous Provençal. "What says Sir Hugh?"

"The emperor tarries," mused the young knight, without turning his head. "When the Greeks come forth from the ravine there will be confusion in their array. At that moment well might the Saracens charge and do us harm."

The silence of the older nobles showed their assent and understanding.

"The emperor tarries," went on Sir Hugh quietly,

The Saracen horsemen
engulfed the remnant of the Franks.

"and so must we go forward to clear his path. Mark ye, messers, that the Saracens hold broken ground. They have left us the heavy sands to cross, the height to climb. Their real strength lies beyond our sight."

"And so," quoth the dour Norman, "it were well to abide the coming of the Greeks."

"Not so!" Sir Hugh shook his helmeted head. "If the foe be in such strength, they can pass around us, and climb to the sides of the ravine, trapping the emperor and his followers."

And the youth in the imperial armor tightened his rein, trotting along the line of knights and men-at-arms, standing full armed by their chargers. Behind him three Normans bore the standard of Theodore, a purple banner surmounted by golden eagles.

Now when he wheeled at the end of the line, a low murmur grew to a joyful muttering. Not a man in the ranks but knew the bay horse he rode, and they who first perceived that this was not Theodore Lascaris but their comrade-in-arms passed the word back to others, until the groups of archers, leaning on their short halberds, were aware that Sir Hugh was in command.

Silence was broken by a roaring shout as men got them to saddle and took lances in hand. Sir Hugh wheeled his bay charger and paced slowly down the slope. No need to race the horses through the sands.

The short line of mailed riders extended no farther than the center of Kai-Kosru's forces. Sir Hugh knew well the danger of thinning his array to try to meet the wide-flung wings of the Moslems. His lances were in the first rank, the axes and swords in the second, and, walking beside the horses, the hooded archers, with strung bows, arrow in hand.

They descended to the rock-strewn bed of the stream, and picked their way across before the Moslem riders had perceived that this was an attack and no change of position.

At once a shrill clamor of kettle-drums and cymbals arose from musicians hidden in the gullies. A blare of the crusaders' trumpets answered the challenge, and clouds of light-armed bowmen galloped down, to wheel and dart around the Franks. Arrows whirred into the mailed ranks. But the archers of Sir Hugh made such response with their long shafts that the skirmishers kept their distance.

Then with a roaring ululation and a thunder of hoofs, a flood of Moslem swordsmen swept over the crest of the ridge, and made at the foremost knights.

"Forward — the lances!"

Sir Hugh turned in his saddle to shout, and, lowering his heavy spear, put spur to the bay charger. The horses of the crusaders broke into a trot that quickened to a plunging gallop before the wave of Moslems struck them.

His feet thrust deep into the stirrups, his body rigid behind close-gripped shield, Sir Hugh glimpsed faces

that swooped down and passed him. His spear drove
back against his shoulder, and he freed the point from
the body of a man, swinging it fairly into the round
shield of a bearded son of Islam, who was galloping
down on him.

The long steel point picked the rider from the
saddle, and the horse careened against the iron-plated
chest of the bay charger. Dropping his spear, Sir Hugh
whipped his sword free, and glanced from side to side.

The wave of Moslems had broken upon the line of
spears and — except where single riders wielded simitar
against sword or mace — had scattered into fragments
that drifted away under the sting of the long shafts that
flew from the bows of the veteran archers.

"Ha — messers!" Sir Hugh laughed, rising in his
stirrups. "Pass forward, and strike!"

He broke through a fringe of dry tamarisk, and
galloped out upon the crest of the ridge, seeing in that
instant the full power of Kai-Kosru.

Before him stretched a wide level where two bat-
talions that had been reining in impatient steeds now
launched against the Franks — two masses of horsemen,
mailed from knee to throat, and splendidly mounted.
He saw that one of these groups were Turkomans, lean
men in white and black *khalats* — the other, the sultan's
Seljuks, glittering in peaked helmets and inlaid mail,
poising javelins as they advanced.

Swinging up his shield, he parried and cut with his

sword, aware of men behind him who thrust with spear and blade, and of the joyous shout of battle —

"For Christ and the Sepulchre!"

The mass of agile riders hemmed him in, and he was struck upon the helm and shoulder. Blood from his forehead dripped into his eyebrows and he shook his head to clear his sight. The Moslems were pressing against the standard and the man they had singled out as the emperor.

But Sir Hugh, putting forth the utmost of his strength, advanced through them, his long sword lashing aside up-flung shield and battle-ax. And the Normans, on rearing, screaming horses at his heels, kept pace with him. No rush of the lighter Moslem horse could stem that steady advance of the close-drawn ranks on level ground.

"Brave blows!" cried Marcabrun, at his side. "They stand not. Let us go on, to where the sultan abides."

"Stay!" ordered Sir Hugh. "Archers to the center. Rein back your men, Sir Clevis! Stand here!"

The masses of Moslems that had drawn off sullenly were joined by others that emerged from the gullies and advanced on the crusaders. On a distant knoll Sir Hugh beheld the green banner of the sultan, Kai-Kosru, surrounded by warriors who had not been in the fight as yet.

"The Greeks come to the valley!" Marcabrun pointed across the bed of gray sand, at the ravine behind

them where some scores of the emperor's spearmen
were visible. Sir Hugh watched them for a moment,
searching in vain for the helmets of Theodore's nobles.
If the emperor's host advanced promptly, it could join
the Franks and occupy the ridge. The crossbowmen of
the Greeks could clear the gullies and the sultan's center
could be broken by a timely charge. The Moslems were
wavering.

This was so clear to Sir Hugh that his heart burned
with impatience, and he caught up the orifan, the long,
curved horn that could send a blast across the tumult of
battle. Once and again he sounded the rallying note that
the Greeks *must* hear. The men about him, with souls
intent on the work in hand, heard the horn and shouted
gleefully:

"Strike, sir brothers! The field is ours."

But above the clashing of steel, the neighing of
horses and the splintering of wood was heard the drone
of the hidden drums, the clangor of the cymbals.

At first the crusaders had broken up the rushes of
the Saracens by countercharges. For the most part, their
spears had been broken and they fought with sword and
mace. Most of them were bruised and bleeding, and all
of them suffered from the burning heat that made the
steel upon their limbs a torment, and sapped the might
of their sinews.

Kai-Kosru's Turkomans had crept up the ridge on

all sides, taking advantage of boulders and cross gullies that protected them from the onset of the dreaded horsemen. With their powerful bows they picked off the horses of the Franks, and the shafts of Sir Hugh's few archers did not avail to drive them back.

By mid-afternoon the crusaders ceased sallying forth and contented themselves with holding the high ground in the center of the ridge.

"Verily," quoth Rinaldo, pulling off his helmet to cool his forehead for an instant, "Satan spews forth these companies of paynim. The cursed fellows rise out of the earth. Hark to their music! Ho, they come again. Make way!"

He thrust forward, urging on his men, until his horse was killed under him by an arrow, and he fought on foot. Sir Hugh noticed him, and reined aside to get between him and the Moslems who were driving in his men. The reckless giant had let fall his helmet, and before Sir Hugh could reach him, a Turkoman had leaned down, an arrow quivering in his fingers.

The shaft struck Rinaldo between the eyes, and the bowman's horse knocked him to earth. One of the Franks slew the Moslem, and Sir Hugh took his stand by the fallen chieftain, bidding those who were nearest carry the body back to the standard.

He looked around, seeking the Norman baron in vain. Marcabrun was casting away the stem of a broken sword, and calling for a new one. Now that Rinaldo and

the Norman were gone, no one remained to give wise
counsel to the young chieftain.

The sun was sinking toward a line of purple hills,
and the hot breath of the sandy gullies rose into the faces
of the surviving Franks. More than half of them lay out-
stretched on the hard, shelterless earth, dead or sorely
wounded. The sun was in his eyes when he looked back
at the ravine from which he had come that morning, and
he could not tell whether the Greeks were moving at
last to his aid or not. But Sir Hugh no longer hoped for
succor from the emperor.

A glance down the ridge showed him that the
Saracens had lost three and four men to his one, but so
great were their numbers that their force seemed unim-
paired by four hours of battle.

And now the sultan Kai-Kosru took matters into his
own hand. His green banner was seen advancing toward
the remnant of the Franks and in that clear, level light of
late afternoon the sultan himself was visible, mounted
on a white Arab courser, bearing a target ringed in black
and gold — a slender, bearded man who looked ever
steadfastly toward the height upon which stood the
wearied bay charger of Sir Hugh.

Around Kai-Kosru trotted his bodyguard, two thousand Seljuks still unwearied, and more than eager to
end by a single charge the long affray wherein such
losses had been inflicted on their fellows.

Beholding this, Sir Hugh knew that two alternatives

remained to him. He could close up ranks and try to cut his way through to the ravine where the Greeks stood, or he could risk everything in one advance upon the sultan.

Swiftly he took account of the numbers of the enemy, and decided that it was vain indeed to draw back now. His little company, harried and beset, would never survive the long march to their allies — and to turn about would discourage his men, and hearten the Saracens. Not a hundred horses remained fit to carry riders.

So thinking, he bade an archer cut the lashings of his helm, and sighed with relief when the hot steel had been cast aside. Shaking back the mail hood from his head, he held up his sword arm and called to his comrades in the brief moment of quiet when they became aware of the oncoming mass of riders and looked to him for an order.

"My brothers, well have you sped this day. You have struck good blows. If we turn back some few may win through; yet if we turn again upon the Saracen, we shall break the sultan's last array, or die with our faces toward the tomb of the Lord Christ."

"Yea, we will go with you, Sir Hugh!" cried the nearest, and even the wounded raised a faint shout of approval.

There was no flinching, no glancing back toward the valley. The men on foot closed in among the horses, and they that limped and panted caught at stirrups to steady them. Tortured by thirst, silent, and afire with grim determination, they moved down the eastern ridge.

So the watchers on knoll and cliff beheld a dark cluster of Franks move onward, into the rush of Kai-Kosru's guards. And, as the waters of a torrent sweep around immovable rocks, swirling and breaking into foam, the Saracen horsemen engulfed the remnant of the Franks.

The bay charger flung up its head, stumbled and sank beneath Sir Hugh, who freed his feet from the stirrups and fell clear, staggering on aching legs. There was a haze of dust about him, and he felt men lurch against him, until a hand pressed his shoulder heavily and he looked up into the bloodless face of the Provençal ministrel.

Marcabrun swayed in the saddle, leaning upon his young comrade. His eyes were sunk in his head, and his cracked and bleeding lips mumbled words:

"A horse for thee, Sir Hugh — God shield thee! I go" — he coughed and gripped the charger's mane with blood-stained fingers. *"Mea culpa — "*

It was a groan rather than a prayer. The broken shaft of a javelin was embedded in one of the rents of his hauberk, beneath the straining chest.

Sir Hugh caught the body of his friend as it slid

from the saddle. Marcabrun's songs were at an end and he had spoken his last brave word. But Sir Hugh never mounted to the minstrel's saddle. A group of foemen burst through the ring of men-at-arms around him, and as he let fall Marcabrun's body, he beheld the white courser of the sultan Kai-Kosru rearing, and black hoofs lashing out at his head.

Kai-Kosru was crouching in the saddle, a heavy simitar upflung in his right hand, which was toward Sir Hugh. There was not a moment between sight and the blow that flashed down at his bare head, but in that instant of time the young chieftain was aware of the gold chain that linked the sword to the sultan's wrist — of precious stones that flared and sparkled in the Moslem's turban knot — and of exulting brown eyes that were fixed avidly upon him.

Then he flung up his shield. Kai-Kosru's blow, descending with the full force of arm and body, and the impetus of the dropping horse, struck fairly upon the shield, cracking it asunder, and knocking Sir Hugh to the earth. But as he fell the crusader cut upward with his long blade, slashing the sultan's knee and the tendon in the courser's off foreleg.

His left arm hampered by the fragments of the shield, and his bruised shoulder numb, Sir Hugh rolled over, and found himself prone beside Kai-Kosru. The

Moslem chieftain had fallen from the saddle when his
horse sank under him, and, maddened by pain, lay on
the earth.

"Yield thee, paynim!" cried Sir Hugh, catching the
sultan's sword arm in his left hand.

Kai-Kosru spat savagely into the youth's bleeding
face, and let fall his simitar to pull a long-hilted dagger
from his girdle. With this he stabbed several times at Sir
Hugh's throat, only to have the slender blade thrust
aside by the right hand of his foe, protected by its chain
mitten.

Writhing back, and freeing himself from Sir Hugh's
grasp, the agile Moslem gripped again his simitar hilt,
bound to his wrist by its chain. Uprising on one knee, he
whirled the curved blade about his head.

But in this second of respite Sir Hugh struck his
adversary between the eyes with his mailed fist. Mighty
sinews were behind the blow and the slender Moslem
sank back with a groan.

Sir Hugh slipped the loops of his broken shield,
and grasped his sword again, striking swiftly. The blade
passed under the beard of Kai-Kosru, and bit through
his neck, into the ground.

In another moment — before the Moslems, who had
drawn back and reined in their horses for fear of
harming their sultan, could do more than cry out in

horror — Sir Hugh grasped the severed head by the beard and hurled it among his enemies, with a wrathful cry —

"Dead is Kai-Kosru!"

A horse, darting upon him from behind, struck him with its armored shoulder, driving the breath from his lungs and the sight from his eyes. He staggered and fell on one knee, powerless to rise or behold what passed above him.

Then, leaping through the rearing horses came a figure panting and yelling, and in semblance more demoniac than human. Its bristling head was red as the blood that ran from its fingers and loins, and in the deep glow of sunset its whole grotesque and powerful body was dyed crimson.

And with knotted, hairy arms this figure laid about it, dealing blows with a seven foot staff of iron bound upon wood, shattering the steel blades and the leather targets of the infuriated Moslems, until they drew back, crying —

"*Div — div!*"*

Then was heard the blast of a hundred trumpets of the Emperor Theodore, who was leading forward his companies of nobles and slaves of Tatar bowmen, and

*A demon.

Bulgar axmen, and the cavalry of the Greeks.

Stunned by the death of their sultan, and wearied by the long combat with the Franks, the host of Kai-Kosru, scattered among the ravines by the river, made little resistance to the Greek attack. They separated into groups, each seeking its way from the field, some swimming the river, some galloping back to Antioch, leaderless.

Thereupon came Theodore, to ride over the field with his captains and councilors, and to look at the chivalry of the Franks, the dead men that lay from the bed of the valley to the ridge and from the ridge to the small ravine where Marcabrun's body was found, scarred by hoofs.

But the body of Kai-Kosru was not found, because the Turkomans had carried it off with them. And, though Theodore, the shrewd and far-seeing, promised rich reward to the man who should bring him the body of the mock emperor, no trace of Sir Hugh was discovered, other than his dead charger and the imperial helmet he had cast away in his last advance.

There was not a moment between sight and the blow that flashed down.

CHAPTER III

When Sir Hugh's sight cleared and the blood left his throbbing temples, he was aware of silence and of shadows. The sun had set, and though the sky overhead was a shimmering blue, the defile was in semi-darkness.

A score of bodies lay near him, and one had been his comrade Marcabrun; but the headless corpse of Kai-Kosru was not to be seen. Only one living man was in the gully, an ungainly form seated on a boulder, a long staff across its bare knees.

Striding toward the stranger, the youth halted to stare at his clumsy armor of iron plates lashed together, the half of them sliced from his shoulders, and at his restless, gleaming eyes.

"What man are you?" he demanded.

"Donn Dera."

"Where are my followers?"

"Raven meat, and so they will lie. There is no help for that."

65

Leaning on his sword, Sir Hugh bent his head. It seemed impossible that all the Franks could have perished; in the desperation of the last struggle he had been able to see only what happened within arm's reach. Where were the Saracens? He asked Donn Dera this, and the strange warrior looked up craftily at the sky. His voice was husky and Sir Hugh thought he had heard it before.

"The war-bands have taken to fleeing," said Donn Dera. "They are fleeing before the incoming of the Greeks. There has been a destruction of many men."

"The Greeks! Has Theodore come upon the field?"

"Yea," responded the stranger. "He has taken up the standard that you let fall."

Again the youth's temples grew hot and he drew a long breath. Turning away, he strode unsteadily down the defile until Donn Dera's heavy hand on his shoulder checked him.

"What now?"

The stranger shook his head.

"It is clear that you are going to confront the emperor himself, and there will be ill words and an end of the matter. You are a fool, though you do not lack courage. Being wise, the Greek will slay you with poison or in other fashion, that no ancient men or minstrels may say he did not keep faith this day."

"Eight hundred men died this day!" cried the youth,

beside himself. "He — he is the one to answer for it."

"In his own fashion he fought," responded Donn Dera grimly. "And surely now, it was you who led your followers into their destruction."

The blood drained from Hugh's cheeks and his hands clenched the leather-bound hilt of his long sword. Donn Dera shook his shaggy head moodily.

"Yea, overyoung you are to be a chieftain. Another time it will fare worse with your foes, better with your followers. Come, we must hide."

Hugh could only look upon him silently. His wearied brain ached.

"Messer Donn Dera," he said thoughtfully, "it is in my mind that you shielded me when I was on my knee among the horses. So may you say to me what would bring harm upon another."

The stranger raised one shoulder.

"What is done is done, and the black shame upon Theodore. Now, a while agone I was spying and peering, and saw the Greek spearmen going about the field putting their weapons into the wounded Franks."

At this Hugh tried to shake himself free of the man and make his way toward the emperor's men, but the hand on his shoulder was not to be put aside.

"Come," whispered Donn Dera again.

"Whither?" Hugh laughed hoarsely. "To the Arabs?"

"Better than the Greeks," nodded the stranger. "The river is best. We must drink."

Hugh suffered the warrior to lead him back through the gully. Donn Dera seemed to have a dog's sense of direction, or a nose for water. Presently the young knight looked down at the ungainly figure, and at the iron-bound staff.

"What is your lineage, and whence are ye, Donn Dera?" he asked.

"I am a man of weapons, and I follow the war-bands and the hosts. Yea, I am quick at rapine and plunder."

"Whose son are ye?"

"The son of Etil, son of Tara."

Although Hugh had never heard these names before, and although he wondered from what land the stranger came, he put forth his hand and said frankly —

"I am beholden to you, Donn Dera, for my life, and while I live this shall not be forgotten."

The man of weapons merely grunted, yet he did not look displeased. The hand that closed around Sir Hugh's was like an iron claw. In silence they pushed through the dense willow growth until they descended a steep slope and dropped among the rushes of the Meander's bank. Then they drank greedily from cupped hands, and plunged steaming heads into the muddied water.

Abruptly Donn Dera clucked and raised his hand. Above them horses were crashing through the underbrush at a mad pace. The man of weapons glanced around, and motioned his young companion to squat down where the tall rushes grew thickly.

Instead of turning aside along the upper bank, the horses came directly toward the river, and in a moment more a score of them slid down the declivity and plunged about in the slippery footing.

Hugh saw that these were Moslems who wore pointed helmets from which hung linen hoods that hid everything except their eyes. They were armed with light spears, slung upon their backs, and simitars. Black cloaks enveloped their slender bodies, and he thought they were neither Turkomans nor Seljuks. Their steeds were nimble-footed and splendid, and these men he had not seen in the battle. They were trotting straight upon him.

Fight was useless, and concealment hopeless. The light along the river was stronger than in the defile above, and he stood up, grasping his sword with both hands.

"Back to back, Donn Dera!"

He moved to where the ground was a little higher and firmer, so that the water came no more than to his knees, and his companion followed him.

The leading Moslems reined aside in surprize. Then, seeing that only two Franks stood in the rushes, they drew forward their spears and rode in upon the twain.

Hugh felt the rugged shoulders of Donn Dera

making play behind him, and heard the snapping of spear shafts. A man cried out and horses reared and plunged. For his part, he cut and parried with instinctive skill. He was over-weary, but so great was his strength and quickness of eye and hand that no spear touched a vital part in him. Glancing steel points slashed him across thighs and arms and his blood ran down into the muddied water.

"Mash'allah!" cried one of his assailants.

The riders drew their swords and exchanged swift words, preparing to rush upon him with their blades. At this moment three other horses crashed down the slope and trotted into the group about Hugh.

One of the newcomers took matters in hand at once. Flinging a question at his companions, he advanced close to Hugh and peered down at him. This was a man lean almost to emaciation. He bestrode a splendid gray Arab, sitting the high saddle with the thoughtless grace of one bred to horses. The trappings of the saddle were cloth-of-gold. Above the black veil that hung from his helm, deep-set, sparkling eyes surveyed the youth.

"Yield thee!" exclaimed the stranger in fair French. And to his companions he added as he noticed Hugh's armor, *"Padishah roumi* — the emperor of the Greeks!"

The Arabs exchanged glances and lowered their weapons.

"I yield to no paynim!" cried the young knight defiantly.

Donn Dera edged closer to him. The man of weapons had been fighting warily, and without the sheer berserk rage that had gripped him during the battle. He, too, was tired. Frowning, he weighed chances. Before Hugh could move, he had lifted his heavy iron-bound staff and whirled it down on the flat of the crusader's sword.

The blow, quick and savage, did not strike the weapon from Hugh's hand, but the steel blade snapped and the point shot from it into the water.

"Take him — thou," croaked Donn Dera to the chieftain of the Arabs. "There is no help for it."

And he cast away his staff, into the rushes. The rider of the gray horse scanned him curiously.

"What man art thou?"

Donn Dera folded bleeding arms across his heaving chest.

"I am a son of a king. Yea, of Etil, son of Tara, overlord of Erin and the grandest monarch of the earth."

The Arab signed to the men who waited behind Hugh, and when the crusader raised his broken stem of a sword, they leaned forward, gripping his wrist. Weakened by loss of blood, he tried to twist free, and then stood quiet, knowing that further effort was useless.

Thereupon the chieftain dismounted from his gray courser and led forward through the mud and broken rushes two riderless horses, ready saddled.

"Khoudsama!" He held out one rein to Hugh. "My

Lord, I am Khalil, the Bedouin. Verily, we are here three princes, and — there has been enough of slaying this day. Come with me!"

Hugh looked into the dark eyes, and in silence gave up the broken sword. The Arabs helped him into the saddle, while Donn Dera mounted. Surrounded by Khalil's men, they swam the mid-current of the Meander, and climbed the far bank, unseen by the sentries of the Emperor Theodore because the sudden darkness of the southern plains had covered the river.

The droning of flies and the *swish-swash* of something moving over his head woke Hugh of Taranto from feverish sleep. He opened his eyes and saw that the moving thing was a fan of heron's feathers, held by a slim hand. The hand emerged from a loose black sleeve, and the sleeve was part of a fragile girl who knelt by his side.

A loose veil, running from her ears to the bridge of her nose, concealed all of her face except two very tranquil and dark eyes and a smooth white forehead.

Hugh stretched out his hand toward an earthen water jar that stood beside him, and the girl raised it to his lips, and held it until he was satisfied. Then, with a half-friendly, half-curious glance, she rose and left his sight. An Arab warrior came and squatted down in her place.

Hugh lay back and began to think. He was in a small tent, of loose, dark wool, supported by a single pole and by what seemed to be the shafts of spears. Under him was a mat of dried rushes, and the sand beneath had been hollowed out to fit his body. His mail and leather gambeson had been removed and a sleeveless tunic of fine white linen, beautifully embroidered, and a coarse brown cloak covered him.

He was alone in the tent with the squatting Arab, and the water jar, but he heard camels sighing and grunting and smelled horses. Through the open flap of the tent he saw high, tufted grass, and naked children playing with goats.

Suddenly he groaned aloud and the warrior looked at him in surprize. But the knight was not feeling the ache of his open wounds; he had remembered the battle of the Meander, and that his comrades Marcabrun, and Rinaldo and all the Norman chivalry were being eaten by crows and wolves. He did not think that the Greeks who had slain the wounded, would give them fitting burial in consecrated ground. And this thought brought the blood to his forehead.

"Khalil!" he said to the warrior. "Take me to Khalil."

Although the Bedouin had not understood the words of the knight, he recognized the name of his chieftain. Nor did he try to restrain the wounded youth. If the Frank wished to go and speak to Khalil, that was his affair. He did bring Hugh the stained and wrinkled leather jacket, and the sword belt, adorned with silver plates, from which the empty leather scabbard still hung. This Hugh girded on and went forth, moving slowly because he was in pain and weak. It had been three days since they swam across the Meander, and all the first day they had kept the saddle.

Hugh thought they had come twenty leagues, south from the battle-field. He did not remember seeing this village, because they had come in at night and he had been asleep.

The village was really an encampment, where women and children tended the goats and camels, and the jars of milk. It was near the hour of sunset and Arabs were rising from the evening prayer, gathering their cloaks about them, and talking in groups. They were thin men, who moved with the grace of animals and looked at the knight with pride.

Hugh noticed that the camp itself was in a grassy hollow, where a rushing stream gave water, and only the wooded summits of distant mountains were visible against the sky. The air, too, was cool, and he thought that these Arabs had chosen a place of concealment far up a mountainside. In the horse herd were more than a hundred beasts, and the saddles standing between the tents were of Turkoman and Greek make as well as the narrow Bedouin saddle.

Khalil, the chieftain, separated from a throng of
warriors and advanced toward him.

"Honor and greeting to the emperor of the Nazarenes!" he said courteously. "Has the fever left thee?
Are thy wounds closed?"

Then Hugh remembered that Khalil had taken him
for the Emperor Theodore, and that their swift flight
from the river must have kept from the Bedouin the
knowledge that the real Theodore was with his victorious host.

"No sultan am I," he made answer in the *lingua
franca*. "I have no rank other than knighthood, and I
am Hugh of Taranto."

Khalil's impassive face was touched by inward
amusement.

"The lord emperor, who is my guest, sees fit to hide
his name and high position. Wherefore?"

"It is the truth."

"In the battle of the Nazarenes and the Seljuks,"
smiled the Arab, "thou wert surely the emperor. Now
it is not otherwise, though a sword is lacking and thou
art the *rafik*, the guest of the black tents."

"My companion, the elder warrior, will tell thee
the truth, even as I have said."

"Thy comrade hath said it — thou art indeed the
emperor."

Hugh frowned angrily. It seemed as if Donn Dera
always did what was least expected of him. He had not

forgiven the wanderer for striking the sword from his hand.

"V'allah!" said Khalil seriously. "Mine eyes beheld thee among the Nazarene weapon men, aye, in the red heart of the slaying. Thy hand slew the sultan Kai-Kosru when a hundred Seljuks hemmed thee in. By the names of Oman and Ali, thou art worthy! I say it — I, Khalil, of al-Yaman, of the Ibna."

Hugh raised his hand impatiently.

"Nay, and again nay! Release me, O Khalil — give me a horse, and the man Donn Dera to attend me. I must hasten to the court of Theodore at Antioch and accuse him before all men. I shall cast my glove at his feet — let him pick it up who will!"

Although Khalil could speak the *lingua franca,* having wandered, like many of his race, from Fez to Saragossa, and even to Venice and Constantinople, he was none too sure what the young knight meant by his words. In all the swift forays of the Bedouins who came up from the desert lands to harry Turk and crusader and Bokharian merchant, he had never encountered a chieftain who allowed another to wear his garments and armor in battle.

So it seemed to Khalil — a master of deception himself — that the captive was trying to conceal his true rank, and making a clumsy job of it. Only one thing puzzled the Arab, who was a judge of character — this royal youth spoke wilfully, and with the appearance of truth.

"Nay, and again nay," the Bedouin made response. "In the battle thou didst bear thyself as a prince — as one, even, of the Three Hundred of Badr. That is truth. Yet, having taken captive the chieftain of the Nazarenes, I may not give him a horse and release him with only one follower, as if he were a common man."

"What then?" demanded Hugh.

Khalil considered. He had been weighing opportunity and guessing at profit for the last three days. Being a fatalist, he had wasted no thought on his extraordinary fortune in carrying off an emperor. God had given it, and moreover the chieftains of the Nazarenes were not like Moslems. They were accustomed to rush into peril unguarded, to fling off helmets when the sun boiled the blood in them, and to venture into all sorts of places.

"*V'allah!* I shall hold thee for ransom at four thousand *miskals* of gold. That is little enough, for the Greek lords are rich beyond belief. I have seen."

It was Hugh's turn to ponder. Theodore was indeed master of rich cities, and overlord of great nobles. True, the emperor's treasury lacked gold and Hugh had a suspicion that the expedition against Kai-Kosru had been planned to win the loot of Antioch which was the governing city of the slain Seljuk. There would be many *miskals* of precious stones, and rare silks, of elephants' teeth and red leather and chests of gold in the castle of Kai-Kosru.

And — if Theodore took Antioch and looted it — four thousand *miskals* might well be paid to Khalil for the persons of Sir Hugh and Donn Dera. They two alone had survived the slaughter on the Meander, and Theodore, having betrayed the Franks, would risk much to silence their tongues — if his men had put to death wounded crusaders on the battle-field.

Theodore, although emperor, did not hold Constantinople. The crusaders had possession of the imperial city, and there was a truce between them and the Greek emperor in Asia Minor.

If Sir Hugh should survive and reach Constantinople, and tell his tale to Henry of Flanders, commander of the crusaders, he would be believed, against the oaths of eight thousand Greeks. Theodore would find it no very easy matter, in any case, to explain to the Count of Flanders the loss of his eight hundred crusaders. And if the truth were known in Constantinople, the host of the Crosses would harry Theodore through all Asia.

"Send to the Greek camp," Hugh said slowly, "trusted men, a few. Bid them look about and ask if the emperor be not in the camp. Aye, they will see him there. Thus it will be manifest that I am no more than a Frankish knight. *They* will not give so much as one gold piece for my life."

That, at least, was quite certain! But to Khalil, reared amid distrust, and experienced in wiles, this appeared no more than a simple trick to lessen the ransom that was his due, and he said so at once. He even laughed — a rare thing in an Arab — not to mock his captive but to show his understanding and appreciation of the trick.

"Shall I sell to the Greeks their emperor at their price and not at mine? May God forbid! If thou wert captive to the Seljuks who hold Antioch, they would ask three cities, and twenty camel-loads of silver, and a sworn truce, with other matters. Give praise to thy saints that I ask no more than two horse-loads of gold!"

A sudden thought struck the youth.

"Tell me, Khalil. Am I — a Frank surely — the man to be named emperor by the Greeks?"

For some time the Bedouin had mused upon this very question and had arrived at an answer that was quite satisfactory.

"By the beard and the breath of Ali, thou art stubborn as a she camel with unslit lip! Was I not at Constantinople, six years agone, when the Franks took it from the Greeks? Since then I have heard that a Frank rules Constantinople, and surely that is the city of the Greek emperor."

Hugh smote hand into fist angrily.

"Who art thou, Saracen? Whence art thou, not to know that the Nazarene army was led by Theodore Lascaris, an elder man, like a fox in wiles, and a treacherous dog-soul of a Greek!"

"Verily am I a Saracen — a robber," assented Khalil calmly. "With eighty of my tribe I came up from the sands to pillage whomever God sent into my hand."

He glanced around his little camp, and added good-naturedly:

"It was written that I should fall in with the Seljuk Turks as they were mounting for battle. I rode with them to the river and watched events. My men gained a few horses, good and bad, and some saddles and gear."

"Khalil!" cried the youth. "Give me no more than one horse, and a week of liberty. I pledge thee the word of a belted knight that I shall return to this place alone, and become again thy captive."

Among the crusaders such a pledge, no matter under what conditions, would have been accepted. The given word of a banneret* was sacred, and Hugh of Taranto was a youth who had kept his word inviolate.

Khalil also was known by the tribes of al-Yaman to be a very mirror of honor, a lion in bravery, and reckless enough to have been beloved by the Companions of Muhammad. But it did not enter Khalil's mind to let four thousand *miskals* of gold out of his hand for a week. He had experienced the treachery of the Greeks.

---

*A knight of distinction, entitled to a banner. Usually only a long triangular pennon was allowed, attached to the spear tip.

The swish-swash of something moving
woke Hugh of Taranto from feverish sleep.

Considering the anxious gray eyes and the flushed forehead of the youth, it seemed to him that his captive's fever must have gripped the brain.

"Nay," said a voice behind them, "not in a week, or in a week of ages would you return from the Greek camp."

Donn Dera was leaning on a knotted staff that he had cut with his knife, and his narrow, bony face was wistful as he looked at his youthful companion.

"That would not be good," said the wanderer again, and turned to Khalil. "Give us to eat, O Chieftain!"

III

CHAPTER IV

THE CUNNING OF DONN DERA

This was a matter of pride with the Bedouin, that his captives should be entertained and made comfortable. He had the hind quarters of a sheep boiling, for them alone, and since his men could not be expected to serve meat to the Franks, he bade the young girl who had attended upon Hugh fetch them milk that might have been goats' or camels' and was probably a mixture of both — a potation that Hugh merely tasted for courtesy's sake, but which Donn Dera sucked down with appreciation.

"Eh, Lord," he grinned, "wash, wipe, sit, eat, wash, and then talk. But not before. A drawn belly breeds ill talk."

And he ate a whole quarter of the sheep, to Khalil's subdued amazement.

"*Yah Khawand,*" the chieftain exclaimed, "what manner of man is this that gorges as a tiger, and drinks as a horse, and sings so that the children gather around him?"

85

"I know not," responded the crusader under his breath, "save that he comes from a land called Erin by some, Ireland by others and Thule by the astrologers — "

"Erin," put in Donn Dera, wiping his broad hands on a passing dog. He seemed to have the ears of a cat.

"He calls himself a king's son, and a man of weapons," added Hugh coldly in a tone Donn Dera could hear readily enough.

"Aye," nodded the wanderer, "in all the world there is no weapon that fits my hand. Sword handles I have broken — ax shafts I have split. From yew wood and iron I fashioned a club, and now that, too, is gone from my hand."

"I did not know you were so strong," said the youth curiously.

Donn Dera glanced at him sidewise, but saw that the crusader had not meant to mock him. After a moment he stretched out his right hand in which the new cudgel was grasped.

The knotted muscles of shoulder and forearm swelled suddenly, and sinews cracked. Between his quivering fingers the wood of the cudgel creaked and then snapped.

Khalil watched with interest and picked up the short staff when the warrior dropped it. The bark had been squeezed away from the wood, and it was broken.

"*Ai,*" he acknowledged, "no man of mine could do that, nor could I. But edged steel is another matter."

"True," put in Hugh at once, "yet in the fighting at the river Donn Dera stood over me when I fell, though mounted Seljuks hemmed him in. How he lives, I know not."

"There was a fury in me," explained the wanderer quietly. "At such moments my hand wreaks chaos and woe, for my father was a man of the elf-mounds, and in him a power of spells and magic."

They were sitting by then at the fire that had been made for the chieftains by the girl, who fetched woolen mantles against the chill of the night that Hugh and Donn Dera heeded not. After a silence, Khalil nodded understanding.

"Such a man we call *djinn*-possessed. Surely thy strength is uncommon."

Donn Dera, chin on hand, looked into the fire, and his lined, red face gave no indication of his thoughts. Hugh, leaning back against the tent, was moody in spirit.

It seemed to the young knight as if this craggy fellow was indeed a companion of evil beings. Donn Dera had broken the good sword in his hand — had lied to the Arab concerning his name — and now boasted openly and with a loud voice. Anger against Donn Dera was bitter in the youth.

"There is one weapon that will fit my hand," the soft voice of the wanderer went on. "It is a sword, and the sword of the great champion Roland, the knight of Charlemagne."

Idle, such words, Hugh mused. Durandal, the unbroken sword of the matchless Roland, was buried with the hero in some cathedral. Long since — four centuries ago — it had passed from the sight of Christian men.

"Of Roland I have heard," assented the Arab courteously. "My ancestors went against him in Frankistan."

"Men say," went on Donn Dera, "the shining glaive* of Roland is of such weight that no warrior of today may deal a cut with it or raise it from the ground, save with two hands."

"That also my ancestors said."

The voice of the wanderer took on a lilting note and his eyes half closed.

"It was in Nicea, in a hostel, that an ancient man of more fell than flesh sat with me the night. He announced to me that he had been to the Holy Land where the feet of the Lord Christ trod, and there was in his wallet a silver flask and in the flask a hair of Simon Peter, and he swore to me by the relic itself that he had word of Durandal, the shining brand, the sword of Roland."

Donn Dera sighed.

-----
*Sword.

"And so this pilgrim tells of the sword, how it lies in the land of the Saracen folk, hanging in the hall of the sultan Kai-Kosru. And this hall is in the castle and the castle is in Antioch. Now in me there is a longing and a desire to have the grasp of Durandal, and that is why I joined the company of warriors that was making a raid upon Antioch."

"That can not be," said Hugh bluntly. "Durandal never left the hand of Roland. Often have I heard Marcabrun — may God grant him eternal rest — relate the song of it. Hark ye, Donn Dera."

He reflected a moment, and repeated the verses of Roland's death:

"Roland feeleth his eyesight reft,
Yet he stands erect with what strength is left.
That none reproach him his horn he clasped,
His other hand Durandal grasped;
Before him a massive rock uprose —
He smote upon it ten grievous blows.
Grated the steel as it struck the flint,
Yet it break not, nor dulled its edge one dint.

'Mary, Mother, be thou mine aid!
Durandal, my masterless blade,
I may no longer thy guardian be,
Though battle-fields I won with thee!
Never shalt thou possessor know
Who would turn from face of mortal foe — ' "

The resonant words of the song rang forth in the clear voice of the youth, and when he had ended, he turned to Donn Dera.

"So, it was. The hero could not break the blade against the stone, so he placed it beneath him, and lay down, that his soul could pass from his body."

Donn Dera wrinkled heavy brows.

"All that may be; but I also have heard Marcabrun, the minstrel. Surely this Roland was a champion and a good man with his weapon. Yet after he died he could not lift hand against a foe, and the Saracens may well have taken such a sword from under his body." After a moment he added, "Was there not a bit in the song about a Saracen who coveted the blade, and took it with him to Arabia?"

"He was slain!"

"Was it an elf or a ghost, then, that dealt with this Saracen? Surely the song relates that all the Franks lay dead about Roland."

At this Khalil, who had been listening attentively, lifted his head.

"Aye, Lord King, that is truth. I knew not the name of the sword, but among my people there is a legend that the blade of Roland, the Frank, was carried from the field under the Pyrenees, to Saragossa, and thence by sea to the land that was once under the yoke of my people and was just now the kingdom of Kai-Kosru."

Hugh flushed and said quietly:

"It is not good to mock captives, O Bedouin. If I wore a sword I should bid thee to combat, for such words are not to be endured by one who wears a belt."

"*V'allah!* If thou wert sound and hale, I should make proof of thee!"

Khalil's deep eyes gleamed.

"Harken, ye Franks — the matter may be adjudged in another way. Years ago I passed through Antioch, and at the palace of the sultan I was shown somewhat of his treasure — "

He paused a moment to reflect.

"Kai-Kosru was ever wary of his gold, but he showed me a strange sword. It was long, it was heavy, and it was not made in a Moslem land. The blade was broad as thy hand, of blue steel. The hand guard was a cross, inlaid with silver, the pommel a ball of gold, from which the precious stones had been taken. It hung upon the wall behind the carpet where the sultan sat. No single man could lift it down from its place. And the sultan said it was the blade of a Nazarene warrior long since dead. Is this thy Durandal?"

"So was the sword of Roland!" Hugh responded promptly. "O that we had known this thing!"

"It waits the man who will not turn his face from any foe," cried Donn Dera. "By the cunning in me I will possess the sword."

Now it seemed to Khalil that both his captives were out of their minds with fever. But when Donn Dera spoke again Khalil looked upon them with greater amazement.

"And thou, Moslem," observed Donn Dera, "thou art consumed by one thought — to take Antioch!"

Veiling surprize with pretended scorn, the Bedouin asked how, with eighty men, he was to think of mastering a mountain citadel, held by several hundred Seljuks and just now besieged by a host of Greeks.

Closing his eyes, Donn Dera rocked his ungainly body in the smoke above the fire, his lips moving.

"There is a way, unknown to the Greeks. A way through the stone of the mountain, into the palace."

This time the self-control of the Arab failed him.

"Art kin to the *djinn*-folk? That was a secret well guarded by Kai-Kosru. It was his way of escape, if an enemy pressed him too hard."

The wanderer wagged his shaggy head.

"It was in thy mind, Moslem, to lead thy men through the stone of the mountain into the stronghold, when Kai-Kosru had achieved victory over the Franks. It fell out otherwise, for the Seljuks fled like wolves while thy men were picking up horses. Now a scattering of them hold the wall of Antioch."

"Say on," demanded Khalil.

"Ochune! Easy to say! Now there is doubt in thee.

Thy men are few, and, besides, here is the emperor, to
be ransomed. Doubt is in thee."

"True — by the beard and the breath of Ali!"

Donn Dera opened his eyes, and Hugh cried out
impatiently:

"Mad art thou! I am not the lord emperor!"

"Easy to say!" Donn Dera grinned. "What dost thou
desire above all things? To ride in among the Greeks,
aye, to the royal tent, and say thy say."

"That is true," acknowledged Hugh moodily.

"And what do I seek? Faith, naught but the sword,
Durandal. Well, let us go and accomplish what we wish."

"How?" insisted Khalil.

His raid into the Taurus mountains had been
inspired by sheer love of risk and spoil. As the man from
Erin said, he had learned of the two armies that were
bound to meet at the river, and he had left the women
concealed in this spot, riding to the heights from which
he watched the battle.

His plan had been to strike boldly at Antioch, which
would be left almost unguarded if Kai-Kosru drove off
the Franks. Stirred by the brave stand of Hugh's followers, he had drawn nearer the river, until his men had
taken to driving off horses, and he had seen the Greeks
overwhelm the shattered Seljuks. Then Hugh had fallen
into his hands, and before doing anything else he meant
to win a royal ransom.

It seemed to Khalil that the red-haired captive had indeed the gift of seeing hidden things. This being so, he might profit by the gift.

"How — O my guest?" he urged.

"Easy to say. Going alone with thy men against the city, even through the mountain, would bring no good to thee. Fighting within the city would bring the Greeks over the walls."

"Well, what?"

"Make a pact and truce with us. Give us good weapons, and we will make thee master of the castle."

"Ye are but two!"

"Two," admitted Donn Dera modestly, "Yet such men as we are not found elsewhere in the lands of the earth. We shall wreak a destruction upon the Seljuks, even as at the river."

"Why should I trust thee with weapons?"

"Trust *him!*" The wanderer nodded at Hugh who listened in frank amazement. "As for me, how could I turn upon thee, Khalil? Would the Seljuks embrace me as a brother? They would not, and that is easily understood."

Khalil thought this over. It seemed to him now, beyond any doubt, that the strange captive had looked into his mind. He yearned to loot Antioch — he had glimpsed a little of the treasure Kai-Kosru had hoarded so jealously. To be master of that palace on the crest of

the marble mountain, for a night! To root out its corners!
To bear off weapons, ivory and shining jewels!

And, beyond all desire for this spoil, was Khalil's
longing to snatch Antioch from the grasp of two armies.
Both armies lacked a leader —

"It were folly," he mused aloud, with an eye on
Donn Dera, "to risk lives on such a blind path, when I
can have three horse-loads of gold as ransom for this
lord of the Greeks."

"Oho!" Donn Dera hesitated an instant, without the
Bedouin's perceiving it. "The Greeks have not so much
gold or silver among them."

"That, at least, is true!" cried Hugh angrily. "Save
for the trappings and gear of the nobles, there is little
precious metal in their coffers."

"But if they take Antioch?" Khalil mused again.

"They will," quoth Donn Dera readily, "unless we
do. The Seljuks are losing heart." He grinned at the fire.
"Khalil, we will storm the city for thee. Let this royal
youth go among thy men, and when we have finished
with the Turks, do thou talk of ransom to the Greeks —
from the towers."

Khalil was silent a long space, while the girl came
and cast more wood on the embers and the flames
crackled cheerily again. To loot Antioch — to compel a
Greek army to send to Constantinople to ransom their
emperor! The thought filled the desert chieftain with

delight. He no longer doubted, because he saw how he could do this, in his own way.

"What sayest thou to this?" he asked Hugh suddenly.

The young knight lifted his head and smiled.

"To go against several hundred with eighty is no easy matter. Give me three days' rest and a fair weapon, and I will go with thee."

"Wilt thou swear, on the honor of a prince, not to try to escape from my men?"

"I give thee the word of a knight that I will not escape."

Looking at the youth, Khalil decided that he would keep his word, but still the Arab was a little puzzled that Hugh should speak of himself as a knight.

"Swear!" he cried, scenting evasion.

"Then fetch me something in the form of a cross — the hilt of my broken brand."

Khalil struck his hands together, spoke to the warrior who lounged out of the shadows into the firelight, and waited until the stem of Hugh's sword with its valuable hand-guard was brought. Holding this in his left hand, while the Arabs watched with curiosity, the crusader placed his right hand upon the hilt.

"I swear upon this cross that I will not lift weapon against thy men, or thyself during the truce between us, and that I will not forsake thee. Moreover, in God's sight, I swear that I will not go from this land until I have faced the lord Theodore Lascaris, the emperor, and cast his treachery in his teeth."

His eyes half closed and his wide lips drew down at the corners, and Khalil thought there was in this young warrior something of the falcon or wolf. Surely the lord Frank meant what he said, although it was nothing less than madness to swear an oath against himself.

"All things are possible in the sight of Allah," he meditated aloud. "Be thou at ease, my Lord. Another moon will not grow to the full before the Greeks ransom thee."

"Of all things," answered Hugh, "I desire that least."

Donn Dera chuckled under his breath, but the Arab flung up his hands.

"Thou art weary, and the fever — go to thy tent, and sleep."

Hugh wished to talk with Donn Dera apart, but his limbs ached and his veins were hot. He suffered himself to be led away by Khalil's attendant, and while he waited for Donn Dera to come to his tent sank into deep sleep. Khalil, too, left the fire, and the man from Erin remained alone with Youssouf, the warrior who had brought the broken sword.

Donn Dera, apparently, never slept. Looking through the smoke at the motionless Arab, he said softly, as if giving tongue to his thoughts —

"Yea, the day comes, and there will be a rare feeding of ravens and whetting of sword edges — there will be sorrow and blood that the wolves will drink."

This prospect was rather pleasing to the warrior of al Yaman, particularly as he firmly believed the speaker had the gift of sight into hidden things, and he asked Donn Dera to prophesy whether the issue would be favorable or not.

"God knows," responded the wanderer.

The Arab nodded, in complete agreement.

"With Him are the keys of the unseen."

CHAPTER V

If a chain is on the lion's neck, the jackal will range the ruins all night long. — Arabic Proverb.

The third day dawned clear and cloudless in its heat, and Khalil waxed impatient. Hugh's fever had left him and his hurts had mended, and it was decided to move toward Antioch.

The horses were driven in from pasture by the boys of the tribe, and the men selected their mounts — Hugh picking out a bay charger that looked as if he were accustomed to a heavy rider in armor. Then Khalil led them to where plundered weapons were kept.

Swords — of the weight that would suit the crusader — were lacking, and the knight of Taranto selected an ax with a curved edge and a pick at the other end. The handle of the ax was three feet in length, of gray ash, smooth and oiled. Donn Dera raked over the pile, grumbling, until he grinned and held up an iron flail —

two-foot lengths of wood and metal hinged together, the tip set with spikes.

"That will not cut a shield," Khalil remarked.

"It will break bones," responded the wanderer.

No shields had been taken by the Arabs, or helmets, and Hugh gave to Donn Dera the mail shirt, sleeveless, that he had worn under his hauberk. At first the man from Erin would not accept this but when Hugh reminded him that he was defenseless against arrows without it, he put it on.

Hugh had been watching the Arabs. They carried light leather targets, slung to slender spears at their shoulders. Each man had his simitar girdled high, as his hands rested among the hilts of numerous and varied daggers — some even wore two swords. Long kaftans and cloaks covered their mail and light steel helmets. They wore no spurs, and managed the horses by knee and voice.

"They move like foxes," said the youth, "swift and alert — but ready to flee as well as strike. How will we storm a gate with such as they?"

"That remains to be seen," admitted Donn Dera, "but if the gate be open, they will slip through like elves."

It was the first time that the crusader had been able to talk with Donn Dera. Hitherto, when he had sought the man of weapons in the camp, Donn Dera had been out with the watchers, or off somewhere with Khalil. The red warrior had the gift of tongues and could make , himself understood more easily than Hugh.

"I know now," said Hugh frankly, "that you broke my sword to keep me from death — though at the time it angered me. But what reason is there for lies? You have made Khalil believe that I am the lord of the Greeks, and you have boasted overmuch."

"That is my nature," explained Donn Dera gravely. "As for the lie — if Khalil understood that you were no more than a young lord of the Franks, he would ransom you for fifty pieces of gold to Theodore Lascaris, who would pay readily enough. Would it please you to stand as a prisoner before the nobles of the emperor?"

"Aye, so that I could face him with his treachery!"

Donn Dera only puckered his lined face, and inspected the hinge of his flail.

"It may be," he said after a while, "that the Greeks can not or will not find a ransom of two men's weight in gold. That is your safety."

"You have the gift of foreknowing," assented Hugh -calmly.

"Not so. I have cunning, and eyes and ears. Youssouf ben Moktar, who is lieutenant to Khalil, speaks the *lingua franca.* Yea, he is almost as great a boaster as I. From him I learned that Khalil covets the spoil of Antioch. And this is a strange city."

"How strange?" asked Hugh, not quite convinced that his companion could not look into the future.

Donn Dera twisted in the saddle. He rode not with the steady seat of the crusader or the pliant ease of the desert men, but with a jerking and shaking of his mighty limbs.

"Well, the Lord Joseph* and I fared forth together two days agone to a height whence we looked down upon the city. He did this because I dared him to go with me while I cast a spear over the wall of Antioch.

"Thus, from a shoulder of these mighty hills, we beheld the city, and it lies in a valley at the end of a lake, like Lough Neague. A small river runs down the valley into the lake, and on either hand of the river are two stone mountains, like giants. Now the town of Antioch runs down the slope of a hill — the one on this side of the river.

"The castle itself sits at the crown of the hill, and its walls are white stone. Now, look. Behind the castle, guarded by its walls and the steep of the hill, is the quarry from which this stone is taken. The quarry eats into the stone summit as a wolf gnaws into the flank of a dead cow. All this we saw, for we left the horses and climbed and peered. We climbed to the end of the castle wall, and cast two spears over it."

---

*Youssouf.

"And what of the path that is to lead us into the castle?"

"Joseph, the Arab, said there was a way through the stone of the quarry. The lord Khalil had heard tell of it. But what the way is and where it lies, I wit not."

He blinked reflectively, and added —

"Yet horses can pass through it. On the shoulder of the mountain behind the castle we saw their tracks, coming and going. Where the footing was all of loose stone, we saw no more tracks, because the Saracen beasts are not shod."

"They might have been Greeks."

"Not so. The Greek standards are planted in the town, where the emperor builds mangonel and ram to batter the gate and wall. Not even a dog or coat could climb from the town to this side of the summit."

"Why did you throw the spears?"

Donn Dera rubbed a gnarled hand through his boar-like bristle of hair.

"They were javelins of your Franks. When they fell among the Seljuks, the paynim must have feared they were cast down from the heavens by warrior angels. It will be a miracle and an omen, and that will not be a bad thing for us."

Everything Donn Dera did was a matter of impulse, and yet he always had a plausible reason for it afterward. He had gone off on a mad venture, in which he might well have broken his neck or been taken by the Seljuks. And he came back with a clear description of the lay of the castle, and its strength.

Three days ago the two Franks had been captives, disarmed and kept only to be sold to the Greeks by the Arabs. Now they were mounted on good horses, and had weapons in hand. Hugh knew that Donn Dera had arranged this by his cunning. Yet as he thumped about on the hard wooden saddle, and fingered his clumsy flail and grimaced, he did not seem to have an idea in his head.

"You say, Donn Dera," he observed, "that you seek rapine and plunder. Why, then, have you joined the host of the Cross?"

"Easy to say, Hugh. There is more plunder to be had with your crusaders than elsewhere."

Hugh smiled.

"Nay, I am poorer than when I came out of Britain, an esquire-at-arms, and took the Cross."

"Then you are different from most of the lord Franks."

"It is not honorable to belittle such lords as Henry of Flanders, and the Count of Villeharduin."

"They are good men, with their weapons, but with their heads they are worse fools than these Arabs who pray five times a day to their god for a battle."

Donn Dera slapped his horse impatiently.

"Now, look. Years ago your crusading barons started from France and Flanders and England to free the tomb of the Lord Christ from the infidel. They marched to Venice and demanded ships and sailors and stores from the Venetians, who are not of much avail as warriors, but no fools. The Venetians gave ships and stores, and the crusaders pledged payment, not in gold — for they had none — but in services.

"So, for a year and a half they fought the battles of the Venetians, and in the end they stormed Constantinople at the will of the Pope and the Venetians. Again they asked for ships to take them to Palestine. The Venetians said it was the season of tempests, and would not go.

"Instead they persuaded the barons to fight the paynim in Asia Minor, and the Franks — brave fools — did so. Then were they led, at the Pope's behest, to go against the paynim Tatars and Bulgars in the north. When a city was captured by them, they must supply a garrison, for others would not. So for four years they took spoil and fought the battles of the Venetian merchants and the Pope. They left their bones around Nicea and in the Dardanelles, but got no whit nearer the Holy Land.'

"But now — "

"Now came the Greek emperor, who had been driven out of his city by your barons, and was a fugitive in Asia. He came humbly, with offers of a pact and truce, and a mutual venture against the paynim sultan, Kai-Kosru. Though the Greeks had betrayed the Franks not once but a score of times, the fools your barons acceded to Theodore's request, and granted him eight hundred Franks to serve him.

"What happened? Easy to tell! Instead of seeking the Holy Land by way of Antioch, Theodore sought only the gold of the Seljuks, and to make sure of winning a victory, he sacrificed all the Franks in his array. Eight hundred fools, and now the ravens are picking their bones by the river yonder!"

At this, moodiness came over the spirit of the youth, for he saw that Donn Dera's cunning had laid bare the truth. He had taken the Cross with high hopes, and when he set forth on this expedition to the heart of the Seljuk land he had thought that at last he would have sight of Palestine.

"Do you think, Donn Dera," he asked, "that Durandal lies of a truth in the hall of the Seljuk palace?"

"I think this. The paynim folk have a great fear and a dread of the Frankish champions, such as Richard of England and Roland, who was the peer of Charlemagne. Such swords they could not swing in their hands, but they would cherish them from father to son as an honor

and a glory to their name. If they say that they have
Roland's sword, it is the truth."

A mighty longing came upon Hugh to have Durandal for his own. He felt sure that he would have the
strength to wield the sword.

Observing him shrewdly, Donn Dera spoke again:

"I shall find and take Durandal. To that have I set
my mind."

"My life I owe to you," assented Hugh readily, "and
though I desire the great sword above all things, I will
yield it to you if I take it."

"Youngling — " the wanderer laughed harshly —
"you have no hand for such a weapon. If you can grasp it
first — keep it. But I will be the one. There is a feeling in
me that this will happen."

His mood had changed in an instant from kindli-
ness to brooding, and he sighed many times.

"Oh, it is said by the priests, 'They who take up the
sword shall perish by the sword.' I have a boding and a
sensing of ill to come."

Whatever Donn Dera might feel within him, he
gave no sign of it when they halted that night where a
little brown grass grew among a labyrinth of loose rock.
They had climbed steadily and a cold wind whipped
and buffeted their lair, to the disgust of the Arabs.
Khalil would permit no fire to be lighted, and they slept

in their cloaks, rousing at times to listen to the horses cropping the tough grass, or the movements of warriors who were going forth to watch.

The Arabs were in no hurry to take to the saddle again, and when broad daylight came Hugh wondered where they were. All around him grew scattered firs, dwarfed and bent by the wind.

At places he could see down into distant valleys, where brown grain rippled and tossed, and through the mesh of the evergreens he glimpsed the reflection of the sun on a broad sheet of water — evidently the lake of which Donn Dera had spoken.

Near the horses he came upon the remnant of a village — huts built one above another into the mountainside, around a cave that had been walled across with stone and clay. The door gaped open and within was only cold and the rubbish of squirrels and dead leaves. But over the lintel of the entrance Hugh made out a cross hewn in a stone, and some strange lettering.

"Ermenie," quoth Khalil, coming up at that moment. "Armenian. Before the Seljuks conquered this land, it was full of such villaes. Now the Armenians have been sold as slaves, or made to labor in the towns — Antioch, Tocat, Zeitun, or Mosul."

"They were Christians!" cried Hugh.

The Arab merely raised his hand and waved it aside

as if to say that what had happened had been ordained and was not to be altered now.

"Come," said he, "it is time."

They mounted and wound upward, through the firs, and Khalil, who rode in advance, scrutinized closely the marks on the trail. There was only the one trail, because it clung to the shoulder of the mountain, and at times they were forced to edge their horses between the wall of brown stone and a cliff that fell away sheer.

Khalil's lips moved as if he were counting, and he and Youssouf exchanged a brief word.

"Many tens of Seljuks came along this trail two nights ago. There were some women, but no pack animals heavily laden. The Seljuks are dropping away from Antioch, but these are the first deserters, who had not much loot."

Hugh could see that the hoof marks went away from the mountain, but he wondered how the Arabs guessed at women, until Khalil showed him the faint outline of a slipper, where a woman had dismounted to lead her pony around one of the outcroppings of stone — and pointed to a fragment of coral anklet trampled into the ground. He showed the crusader, too, where the Seljuk horses had galloped across a wide slope, explaining that heavily laden animals would have kept to a foot pace.

"If these warriors have their families," he added

shrewdly, "they will not wait to plunder those who come after. They will not wait at all."

When the sun was almost overhead, and its heat warmed the cavalcade in spite of the chilling wind, Khalil dismounted to search the ground. Here a narrow gorge ran back into the cliffs that now rose several hundred feet overhead. And here the chieftain left all his men but Youssouf and Hugh.

On foot, the three leaders followed the ledge around the shoulder of the mountain, and Hugh saw that here were no hoof marks. Soon they were ascending over masses of purple and whitish stone, and leaping fissures. Youssouf led the way around a turning, and climbed a pinnacle of rock with the agility of a goat.

"Antharikyah, dar assiyadah!" he called back softly. "Antioch, the abode of power."

When the others joined him, all three lay down and drew themselves to the edge of the rock.

"V'allah!" muttered Khalil. "We have not come too soon."

In the brilliant sunlight the scene below them, to the left, was etched in minutest detail. Almost abreast them, a bare two arrow flights away, was the castle of Kai-Kosru — a castle built upon a ledge of solid marble, white, with reddish veins running through it. A wall of marble blocks, some twenty feet in height, had been built around it. Above the wall appeared the dome of a mosque, the terraced roofs of buildings and a single slender tower with a watch gallery at the summit.

The ledge was the shape of a half moon, curving out from the summit of the mountain, and so steep was the slope at either side that no men in armor could climb it without aid from above.

So there was no wall at the base of the half moon. Here the eyes of the watchers were dazzled by the glare of sunlight upon pure white marble, and here, Hugh thought, lay the quarry, built into the very crown of the hill. But between them and the quarry was the cliff, a hundred feet high.

He looked again at the castle. Groups of warriors were visible on the wall, plying their bows through the crenels of the battlement. Others stood in the watch tower, and Hugh could hear them shout, one to another.

"How many?" Khalil asked his lieutenant.

"More than two hundred, less than four. I watched, for the interval between two prayers. I saw no women."

"They have been sent away. A few Seljuks went to guard them, and these others remain to carry off the sultan's wealth, if the castle can not be held."

"Would even a few go hence without the wealth?"

"Aye, for they had the women of these as surety." He nudged Hugh and asked, low-voiced, "What think ye of the wall, my Lord — will it fall?"

Hugh could see the flank of the castle, and one end

of the Greek lines. The ledge on which the castle stood was some hundred feet above the highest roofs of the town. And the town itself — brick dwellings with flat, clay roofs, set amid gardens and terraces where red grape-vines grew — descended from the base of the ledge to the river, far below. The streets were little more than stairs.

And these streets swarmed with Greek soldiery. Archers and crossbowmen occupied the nearest buildings and kept up a steady fire at the battlement above them. Other detachments escorted captive Turks who were hauling up massive timbers. The snapping of whips mingled with the whirring of crossbows.

"They have built a counter tower," explained Hugh. "See, they batter down the gate."

Within the vision of the watchers stood a strange edifice. It was wide at the base, narrowing to a summit, on which, reared back like the head of a striking snake, the long shaft of a mangonel was being bent. The wooden tower was fashioned of tree trunks, laid horizontal, and covered with raw hides as a protection against blazing arrows. Men could ascend within it to the platform, which was shielded by mantelets. And these men were levering back the seasoned beam that held a boulder in the pocket at its end. Great ropes creaked, and the beam was suddenly loosed, the stone shooting forward and up.

Khalil, watching with interest, could not see where it struck, but heard the thud of it, and the pounding of marble fragments sliding away. A white dust rose over the wall, and the Seljuks shouted in anger.

"They lack heart," muttered the Arab. "Once we faced such a wooden tower and cast upon it light clay jars that broke and loosed a liquid on the timbers and the men. They mocked us, for they took no hurt from *that*. Then, when all the tower was wet we cast over torches. *Bismillahi!* The liquid was naphtha."

"How is the entrance?" asked Hugh. "Do ladders or steps lead up, or is there a road?"

"A road," responded Khalil, "runs slantwise up the ledge to the gate, which is teak. By it, horses come to the castle. Half-way down the ramp small towers stand and a lower gate, but this the Greeks may have destroyed."

"Then, when the stone caster has battered in the gate, they will assault the ramp and enter through the breach. But they will not attack until a way has been opened."

Khalil nodded assent, thinking that Hugh's interest had been stirred by sight of his men at the siege work, and that the crusader was eager to join the Greeks once more. And when they had climbed down from the rock and rejoined the waiting warriors, Khalil spoke to Youssouf, ordering his lieutenant to follow at Hugh's back with two men, to shield the crusader.

It seemed to the Arab that his captive was eager to go against the Seljuks. And, having witnessed the crusader's recklessness in battle, Khalil proposed to take no chances of losing four thousand *miskals* of gold.

VI

CHAPTER VI

THE WAY THROUGH THE MOUNTAIN

At the end of the first watch of the night, Arab sentries came back from the lookout rock and reported that all was quiet in Antioch. The Greeks had ceased their hammering at the wall.

Khalil glanced at his men, nodded to Hugh, and flung off his white *koufiyeh*. Tightening his girdle, he looked up at the stars and spoke three words —

"Come, my children."

Striding into the maw of the ravine, he was lost to sight instantly, and the three warriors who followed him. Youssouf nudged Hugh, and the two Franks stepped out of starlight into the utter blackness of trees between two cliffs. In their dark armor, with black hoods and skirted tunics, the Arabs were invisible. There was no talk, or blundering together.

At sunset the horses had been sent back along the trail, guarded by five warriors who made no secret of their disgust at this mission.

Hugh, ax on shoulder, his eyes on the vague shape of the man in front of him, advanced up the ravine, feeling his way around the twisted and thorny boles of trees, and sliding down clay banks. At times he walked over the round stones of a dry stream bed.

There was a halt and a muttered challenge when Khalil picked up the two sentries that had gone up the ravine.

Then Youssouf peered into his face and touched his shoulder. Following the lieutenant, Hugh climbed a bank, clinging to the roots that met his hand, and emerged from the brush into a narrow gorge. Through the cleft between rock walls far overhead, he could see the gleam of stars, and a cold wind brushed past him.

"Ah, what is this?" Donn Dera whispered in his ear. "I am thinking that this is neither quarry nor cairn, but a path into a pit, and no good at the end of it all."

Hugh could hear his companion's teeth clicking together, and his breath sighing and the ends of his flail striking against the cliff, and he wondered at the man's anxiety. Donn Dera did not lack courage, but the gusts of wind that whined in the gorge, the silence of the place, made him fearful.

Skilled marauders, the Arabs moved without a sound of footfall or metal striking against armor. Hugh could make out the faint gleam of their helmets. Then he could see nothing before him, and his ax struck stone overhead. He felt up with his hand and discovered that he was entering a tunnel where he could touch the wall on either side. Bending his head, he strode on.

Presently the walls fell away, and the forms of men ahead of him became visible. He was standing in what seemed to be a narrow room, carpeted, without any ceiling. Reaching down, he picked up gritty dust in his fingers. Then he knew that he was in the quarry and that the white walls of the niche were marble.

The Arabs cast about a moment and entered a corridor that was so narrow only one man could pass at a time. This passage turned many times, until the men in advance halted and Hugh was dazzled by the gleam of firelight on the streaked stone.

Pushing up to Khalil, he looked around the corner. There was barely room for one man to squeeze out of the corridor, and the Arabs had halted.

By looking over their heads Hugh could see the fire, in the heart of the quarry. It crackled and swirled under the wind gusts and sent shadows leaping over the gleaming wall of stone. Marble blocks, half chiseled into smoothness, stood at the sides, with piles of ropes and pulleys and hammers, and the short wooden ladders used to climb from ledge to ledge.

Clustered around the fire were some score of Seljuks. Several of them were talking at once, pointing and arguing, and — though they had spears ready to hand

— they had eyes only for one another. A single sentry leaned on his spear and listened, almost within reach of Khalil.

The man was a bearded warrior who esteemed himself not a little, by token of the two swords and array of daggers girded under his ribs, and a Greek shield slung over his shoulders. From time to time he yawned and spat, his beard bristling in amusement at the oaths that flew about the fire. And without warning, aroused by a slight sound, he turned and looked squarely at the Arab who was moving toward him from the corridor.

"Yah hai — " he roared, and reeled back, falling with a clash of steel, Khalil's javelin fast in his throat.

The Seljuks sprang up, groping for weapons. Seeing the warriors running from the passage they closed in on them without waiting to dress shields or string bows.

Khalil, with a half dozen Arabs, met their rush with two-edged simitars, and before Hugh came up the chieftain had shifted his ground. The Arabs seemed to flow, rather than run, from the passage, bending low until they leaped at their foes.

Spreading out to the sides, they pulled down the Seljuks who tried to fly from the quarry. The remaining guards crowded together, then scattered and rushed desperately. But the swift-footed desert men sliced them with the curved simitars, and the cry of *"Aman"* ("have mercy") was raised in vain.

"Yah Khawand — yah rafik!" roared Khalil's men as the last Seljuk went down. Some picked up an extra sword, and they all swept after Khalil, across the floor of the quarry.

At the edge of the firelight they came full upon a chasm or a foss cut where the clay of the castle plateau met the stone of the mountain. It was too wide to leap, and there was no way of telling its depth.

As a precaution — though no attack had been expected from the quarry passages — no bridge had been built across this chasm. Instead, a light beam lay athwart it, and two sentries stood at the far end.

They had heard the fighting and seen the Arabs run from the fire, but, fearing to leave their comrades in a trap, had not pulled back the beam until the first assailants came up.

And these, without a second's hesitation, flung themselves bodily upon the beam, catching it in their arms and holding it in place with their weight. Some of the Arabs rushed across the shaking bridge, and the two sentries fled. The men who now hung to the beam were drawn up, and Khalil's band ran into the heart of Kai-Kosru's stronghold.

Hugh saw that the last man over halted long enough to push the beam loose, and it disappeared into the depths of the mountain.

Somewhere in the darkness kettle-drums sounded,

and a man ran from the door of a palace building waving a smouldering torch over his head. He was cut down before he had a chance to cry out. Darkness favored the Arabs, and Khalil, who knew the plan of the castle, made the most of surprize.

Leaving the dome of the mosque on his left, he ran toward the sultan's dwelling on his right. At the portico a dozen of the garrison had mustered and were shouting at the sentries on the wall, believing that the attack had been from without.

These were surrounded by the Arabs, and their outcry ceased suddenly in a clatter of steel. Guards were at the gate of the outer wall, and some hundred Seljuks were standing at the rampart, kindling cressets, stringing bows and shouting to know what the matter was.

Between the wall and the palace, Hugh made out the foliage of a garden, and the shimmer of water. Beyond the garden stood a low structure that looked like a barrack, and here also there was a bustle and clamor. Calling half of his men to him, Khalil plunged into the garden, and Youssouf cried out to the Franks —

"Come, Lords, we will take the sultan's *serai!*"

Paying no attention to the warriors on the outer wall who fingered their weapons and peered into obscurity, unable to make out friend or foe, Youssouf sprang through the columns of the portico into the tiled entrance hall.

Hither the leaders of the Seljuks were hastening, down the stairway from a balcony, out of corridors. And here there was light, reflected on the gilded ceiling from hanging oil-lamps.

Hugh confronted the foemen who had vanquished his followers a week ago — stocky men, with broad, bony faces, clad in Damascus and Persian mail. By the plumes in their helmets, he recognized several chieftains and made toward them with Youssouf at his elbow.

One of the Seljuks stepped out to meet him, with shield advanced and simitar lifted. Hugh had learned that the light, curved blades of these fighters could strike inside the sweep of an ax. Lacking a shield, he gripped the shaft of his weapon in both hands and sprang aside as the warrior cut at him.

The simitar glanced from the mail coif, laced about his head, but his ax, swung with all the strength of his shoulders, caught the man fairly between throat and arm. Tearing through steel links and shoulder bones, the ax grated against the Seljuk's spine, and he fell prone, bearing with him the embedded ax.

Others leaped at Hugh with a shout of anger, but Youssouf slipped in front of the crusader, and Donn Dera's whistling flail backed the Arab up. Putting his foot on the Seljuk's body, Hugh wrenched out his ax and snatched up the round steel shield that the dying man had dropped.

Outnumbered, the leaders of the Seljuks fought desperately, crying to their followers to come to them. Several of them pressed together and cut their way out of the hall and ran from the palace. The others were pursued through corridors and balconies until they scattered in headlong flight.

"Ho!" cried Youssouf. "These are vultures, and we have stripped their feathers from them."

He kicked a plumed helmet and sent it spinning across the tiled floor.

"Come Lord King, let us see where Kai-Kosru kept his wealth."

"What of Khalil?" demanded the knight.

"Khalil is a hawk, and these are vultures. Come!"

And, regardless of what was happening outside the palace, the Arabs snatched up lamps and torches and spread through the inner chambers. Here the floors were richly carpeted and the marble walls bore paintings of Seljuk sultans and their battles. Youssouf halted in his stride and threw back his head, baying like a hound at scent of quarry.

"By the Ninety and Nine holy names — by the beard and the breath of Ali, the Companion — lo, the vultures have trussed up their meat and left it for the hawks to find!"

It was, perhaps, well for the marauders that the

garrison had been preparing to evacuate Antioch. Had
the Arabs, scenting loot, scattered through the sleeping
chambers and the deserted women's quarters, stripping
and plundering, Youssouf could never have held them
together.

As it was, in dozens of stout leather saddle-bags and
goatskin packs, the treasure of Kai-Kosru and his ancestors lay gathered before their exulting eyes in the center
of an anteroom. More, it was neatly sorted and packed
and the warriors who had been guarding it had fled.

With a slash of his simitar, Youssouf cut the thongs
from the neck of one sack and thrust his hand within.
Under the beards of his companions he held out gold
bezants and heavier coins stamped with Greek letters
and the likeness of pagan gods — Persian *dinars,* bearing
the figure of a horseman.

"*Ai-yah!*" cried Youssouf, delving deeper, "here is a
dirhem of the caliph Aaron the Blessed (Haroun al-
Raschid, of Bagdad) and another of Sal-edin, the foe of
the Franks. Verily, Kai-Kosru had his finger in every
purse of al-Islam. Well, he was a good provider!"

"The praise to the Giver!" echoed a warrior who
was prodding a goatskin.

Others unearthed jewels in the smaller saddle bags
and held them up to the torchlight gleefully, but Youssouf, well satisfied with the extent of the Seljuk treasure,

remembered that the fighting was not over by any means. Hastily he told off ten men who were slightly wounded to guard the sacks.

Then he looked around for the two Franks, at first casually and then more anxiously, until he struck clenched hands against his temples and stormed at his followers.

"Thieves — sons of misfortune — O ye spawn of the gullies! Was the door of plunder open that ye should shut eyes and ears against the two Nazarenes, the captives entrusted to ye by Khalil! Out upon ye — search, seek — "

A shouting at the outer gate silenced him and he clutched his beard when he heard the cry of the Seljuks.

"Yah hai — Allah, il allahi."

Muttering, he gathered together the twenty remaining able-bodied men and sallied forth to learn what was taking place outside the palace.

While the Arabs were crowding around the bags of gold, Hugh looked for Donn Dera. Not finding him in the anteroom, he went back to discover whether his companion had been struck down in the entrance hall. Here was no sign of the man from Erin, and Hugh continued his search, wandering through a corridor that led into the garden court in the center of the palace. This was in darkness, but at the far end a glimmer of light came from between slender pillars.

Hugh confronted the foemen who had vanquished his followers a week ago

Ax in hand, the crusader crossed the garden, circled a marble pool, and advanced through the colonnade. He found himself in the throne-room of Kai-Kosru.

A single oil-lamp brought to life the blue of lapis lazuli set in the wall, the soft sheen of silk carpet underfoot, and the glint of shields and rare swords — simitars, yataghans and daggers hung behind the dais upon which stood the narrow silver chair of the dead sultan.

And beside the lamp on this dais sat Donn Dera with a six-foot sword across his knees.

Hugh came closer and looked at it, knowing that this was the sword Durandal. Its pommel was a gold ball from which the empty jewel facets stared like blind eyes. From pommel to crosspiece extended a bronze bar, long enough for two hands to grip, and the wide crosspiece curved toward the blade like a new moon.

"That is Roland's glaive," he said.

The blade was broad at the base and the bright steel had the glow of silver. Down it ran an inscription that Hugh could not read. The point was blunter than in the swords Hugh had used.

All at once he felt that here was a sword of enduring strength. His hand longed to take it up. He thought that the bronze would fit his hand.

"Yea," quoth Donn Dera, "I found it hanging above the throne. I lifted it down."

The wanderer was gazing at the great blade as if puzzled or grieved.

"I can bend any bow or cast any spear — I can lift this blade above my shoulders, but there is no strength in me to swing the sword Durandal."

"With both hands, then," suggested Hugh, who was afire with eagerness to do that very thing.

"Nay, I have the ache of long years in my joints. The sword is too heavy. Ah — "

Donn Dera stared at his companion in surprise. The young knight had dropped to one knee and clasped his hands upon it. In doing so he had shaken back the mail coif from his head so that his mane of tawny hair fell around his shoulders.

After a moment Hugh spoke to Donn Dera.

"I thank the Lord Christ that we have found the sword of the hero, and will take it from paynim hands."

"Yea, we shall take it," muttered the wanderer. "My cunning found it, though I have not the strength to wield the great sword."

"Come and find Khalil."

Together, the elder walking with effort under the weight of the six-foot blade, they went from the throne-room and garden to the entrance of the palace. Hugh could not keep from looking again and again at Durandal. Donn Dera had found the sword and it was his. But the young knight was glad that it would not fall to the

Greeks. The blade gleamed, in such a friendly manner, as if asking him to take it up.

Theodore had tricked him at the battle of the Meander, had broken the Seljuks, and would be master of Antioch. In all things he was victor because he was shrewd and experienced and knew how to deceive others.

VII

CHAPTER VII

THE GAUNTLET

Utter confusion reigned outside the palace. Rider-less horses plunged away from spluttering torches. Groups of Arabs flitted between lights, and beyond the outer wall of the castle there rose the steady, threatening roar of a multitude. On the wall, Seljuks were loosing arrows from their bows.

But they were sending their shafts into the outer darkness, and half-heartedly, because they were aware of the Arabs in the palace and the stables.

"By Michael," grinned Donn Dera, "the Greeks are attacking the gate."

They saw Khalil then. The chieftain of Yaman was taking full advantage of confusion. Having cleared the barrack of Seljuks, he had scattered his few men so that the garrison on the wall could not judge his strength, and must have fancied in their desperation that all Arabia had descended from the mountain.

Carefully Khalil had counted the defenders of the

wall — a hundred and fifty, warriors and officers. He had loosed the horses to add to their perplexity, having appropriated the best stallion for his own mount, and now, escorted by torches, with sheathed sword and hand on hip, he revealed himself to the harassed Seljuks.

"O ye men of Kai-Kosru!" he shouted in a voice that carried over the tumult. "Are there not souls enough in paradise that ye should stand against the Roumis and join the company of the slain?"

"What man art thou?" one of the Seljuk leaders demanded.

"I am Khalil el Kadhr, chief of Ibna, lord of Yaman. My men hold the palace and what is in it. Lay down your weapons or we shall throw you to the Roumi dogs that bay without!"

Khalil looked both triumphant and satisfied. In reality he was on fire with anxiety. If he tried to withdraw taking the sacks of gold — and Youssouf had told him their worth — the Seljuks would be aware of his scanty numbers, and would turn to fight for the treasure. So far he had not molested the garrison on the castle wall, and the last thing he wished to do was to attack them from below.

Meanwhile the Greeks, aroused by the tumult within, had ventured up the ramp and were beating at the outer gate with a ram. Their crossbow bolts whistled past the Seljuk helmets.

"Nay, withdraw, O ye Arabs!" cried one of the

Turkish officers. "Leave the horses — the infidels will be in upon us before the first light."

Khalil laughed loudly.

"When did the men of Yaman leave horse to the sultan's dogs? We shall deal with the Greeks. Throw down the weapons — now, or we will come against thee with the sword."

Perhaps memory of the dread Arab simitar stirred the Seljuks, or sheer uncertainty made them desperate. They had seen their comrades slain or scattered — most of their leaders were lost, and they were quarreling among themselves.

"Then, Khalil," cried he who had bade the assailants withdraw, "let there be peace between us. We will help thee bear the gold to safety, away from the cursed Greeks. Then will we talk of horses and a division of the treasure — "

"Does the lion sit down with the jackal? I would have left ye, to live — "

"Nay, Arab!" The Seljuk cried out hastily when he saw Khalil turn as if to give an order. In imagination the men on the wall saw a thousand arrows loosed at them, and they all began to shout at once.

"*Aman!*"

"Forbear — we are believers. Have mercy, Khalil!"

"We hear and obey! Only stand back and let us pass into the quarry."

Khalil looked at them without apparent pleasure.

"Then cast down weapons — *all* weapons! The javelins likewise. What, have ye no knives?"

A few at first, scores of simitars, spears and bows clattered on the stones beneath the wall, and the Seljuks ran down the inclines, some prostrating themselves before Khalil's horse. But the Arab wished neither talk nor delay.

Youssouf and bands of the desert men hounded the prisoners off toward the stables, thrusting at them with their own javelins and mocking them. The Seljuks were thoroughly disheartened, and — though many of them had long knives hidden under cloak and girdle — more than willing to flee.

A few of them picked up a stout plank bridge set on rollers that must have been used by the sultan to pass horses across the chasm. Pushing this into place, they fought to be first to cross to the sanctuary of the mountain. When the last had disappeared, Youssouf stationed a guard at the movable bridge and hastened back to where his chieftain was loading horses with the sacks of gold and precious stones that were being carried from the palace.

A warrior shouted and they stopped their work, rigid with astonishment.

Hugh had walked past them to the gate that was already splintered and shaken. One of the iron bars had been knocked down. Setting his shoulder under the remaining bar, the tall crusader lifted it, cast it aside and wrenched open one of the teak doors.

Reaching out his hand, he gripped the sword on Donn Dera's shoulder, and with this he stepped through the opening to confront the mass of the besiegers.

No Arabs were near enough to prevent him, and they who snatched up bows and javelins to slay him remembered that he was Khalil's captive, the emperor.

Below Hugh of Taranto a hundred torches smoked and crackled. Under his feet was the debris knocked from the wall by the stones, and the length of the inclined ramp was littered with fragments of marble and the ruins of the lower towers.

Upon the ramp several hundred Greeks had ventured, and now stood poised, with shields raised over their heads, sword in hand. The nearest, who had been driving a tree trunk against the gate, had let fall their ram and snatched up spears, fully expecting a sally from the opened gate.

On the hillside below were ranks of crossbowmen, covered by mantlets, and on the *bellfroi*, the gigantic tower, were other detachments, mustered under the white and gold standard of the Caesar.

Beyond arrow-flight of the wall, Theodore Lascaris, the emperor, sat a white horse with crimson caparisoning, attended by his Sebastocrators, his chief officer, his councilors and Mavrozomes, the armorer. He had heard that the Seljuks were forsaking the wall and fighting among themselves, and, no sluggard, where an advantage was to be gained, he had commanded an instant assault, lending his presence to encourage the men of his host.

Conspicuous, in his gilded armor and griffon-crested helmet, illuminated by a ring of torches and outlined against the great banner with the purple cross, Theodore was perceived at once by the knight of Taranto. For their part, sight of the tall Frank in the aperture from which they had expected a sally of Turks, filled the Greek soldiers with astonishment. When they noticed the gold wrought mail and the purple cross upon Hugh's ragged surcoat, their bewilderment waxed greater.

They had been told that all the Franks were slain at the Meander, and here was one of the crusaders in the emperor's mail, leaning upon a sword of unearthly size — and Hugh himself, standing upon the pile of debris, his long hair shining in the flickering torchlight, seemed to them of gigantic stature.

So, within and without the castle wall, there fell a quiet in which the crackling of cressets and the stamping of horses could be heard. And in this moment of near silence Hugh raised his hand.

"Lord King — " he cried.

A bolt from a crossbow whirred past his ear and crashed into the stone lintel of the gate.

Hugh's voice now reached to the imperial cavalcade, and even the horse sergeants beyond.

"Down weapons! Sir Hugh of Taranto speaks, who defended the banner and person of the emperor at the Meander — "

He said no more. In Mavrozomes, peering up from the press below, there was a nimble wit. The armorer understood instantly that Hugh had escaped the slaughter at the river, probably as a Seljuk prisoner — Mavrozomes imagined that Hugh had been thrust out by the Seljuks to parley for terms of surrender, and the last thing the Greek nobles wished was that the knight of Taranto should have opportunity to speak before the whole army.

So Mavrozomes reasoned, and acted upon the thought. Gliding to the rank of crossbowmen, he clutched the shoulder of a sturdy Genoese, whispering —

"A purse of bezants — a captain's belt to thee, if thou canst bring down that tall foeman."

Thus the first bolt was sped, and the armorer, cursing its failure, passed to a second man, offering a dozen slaves and two heavy purses.

"Aim lower, at the cross!"

The light was illusive, Hugh's appearance bewildering, and the whisper of Mavrozomes imperative. The other man settled his shoulder against the iron stock and pulled the trigger. The bolt whirled upward, crashed against the knight's light shield and tore through it, but glanced aside. The crusader shook the shattered shield from his arm.

The parley ended as swiftly as it had begun. For the captain in command of the men highest on the ramp had taken account of the two missiles, and, feeling himself in jeopardy, shaded his eyes and looked down at his leaders.

One word passed Theodore's lips and the Sebastocrator heard and lifted his ivory baton, pointing it toward the gate, twice — that there should be no mistaking his meaning. The captain understood and cried to his men —

"At him — through the gate."

Spears lowered, the Greeks advanced. And at this sight fierce anger mastered Sir Hugh. His eyes glowed and he raised the sword overhead.

"St. George!" he cried, and again, "St. George!"

His sword flashed down in a horizontal sweep that snapped off the nearest spearheads, and swept back, as he stepped forward into the boldest of the Greeks. Three men were cast down and lay without moving.

"A traitor!" shouted the captain. "Oho — he is

leagued with the Saracen and the devils of the pit!"

What followed was witnessed by three thousand souls on the hillside below and by as many Arabs as could crowd into the half-opened gate — the sight of whom had inspired the Greek officer's shout.

The ramp was no more than eight feet wide and covered with broken stone, so that only three men could stand upon it abreast. Bending low and shortening their sword arms, the Greeks rushed and were swept from their feet with broken bones and bodies gaping. Some slid off the ramp but they were dead before they touched the ground, a hundred feet below.

"Over the bodies," ordered the captain angrily. "Shield to shield. Thrust with spears from behind."

Three warriors linked shields together and went up, while others who had the long light spears of the foot soldiers pushed their weapons in advance of the three.

"Well done!" laughed Sir Hugh.

He stepped forward, and a spear tore through his cheek, grinding into the bone. His sword smote down the middle man of the three, and he leaped back. An ax clanged against his straining chest as he heaved up Durandal, breaking the links of his mail.

"Well struck!" he roared, and cut inward, toward the rock. The two leaders were knocked against the cliff, their limbs numbed by the impact. Spears snapped.

Hugh fought with the cold rage and the swiftness of

the man who knows his weapon. There was in him at such a moment the instinct of the falcon that strikes only to slay and is not to be turned from its quarry. Aroused in every nerve, his long body and iron muscles wielded Durandal as an ordinary man might swing a staff.

No man struck by that sword rose again. A tangle of bodies lay on the ramp at his feet, and he saw the Greek captain climb in desperation upon the huddle of his men. The Greek, who gripped a shield close to him and a short sword upraised, leaped forward to strike at the crusader's unprotected head.

And as he leaped Sir Hugh took two steps back, swinging Durandal far behind his right shoulder. The six-foot blade whined through the air and checked as it struck the Greek above the hips — then swept out and up to the left, gleaming and hissing.

Smitten in mid-leap, the body of the Greek flew out from the ramp and a shout burst from three thousand throats. The form of the captain divided into two parts, the legs and hips whirling away from the trunk, falling into the line of crossbowmen.

Beholding this, the Greeks on the ramp drew back, and the mutter of voices from the ranks below was like the murmur of innumerable bees —

"May the saints aid us — such a stroke!"

"Take up bows — make an end — "

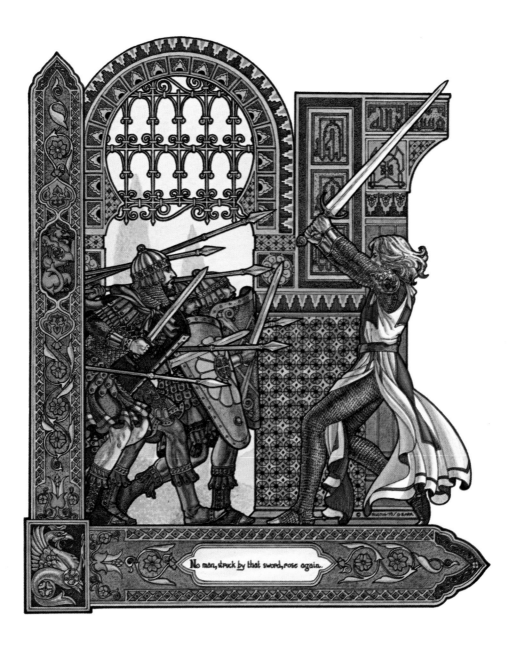

No man, struck by that sword, rose again.

"Nay, what say the nobles? I marked how the first bolts did him no harm — "

"By Sergius and Bacchus, the warrior is more than human. Whence came he? See, there is fire playing around his brow."

This muttering dwindled when Hugh, resting his sword tip on the roadway, drew from his right hand the gauntlet of steel links.

"Theodore Lascaris," he cried, "Lord King, forsworn and traitor. By thy treachery died eight hundred, my companions, who served thee faithfully. Worthier knights than I lie now unburied at yonder river, but I alone am left to proclaim thy guilt, and this I do, challenging thee in thy person or by champions, to do battle with swords that God may judge between us."

And he cast the gauntlet after the body of the Greek captain, so that it circled in the air and fell among the knights sitting their horses below the ramp.

This sudden cessation of the struggle at the gate produced a silence among the Greeks, and they who understood Sir Hugh's words glanced curiously at the emperor. But Theodore Lascaris, his lean face white under the silver helmet, fingered the tasseled rein of his charger, giving no response or any indication that he had heard. Seeing him thus hesitant, the nobles debated whether or no to pick up the gage cast down by the

Frank, and while they hesitated, Sir Hugh spoke again.

"I am the banneret of Taranto, my lineage the equal of any prince of the Comneni. If thou wilt not accept my pledge, name thy champions and I will meet them in this hour upon level ground until one or the other perish."

A strong hand grasped Hugh's belt at the back, others caught his arms, and he was drawn suddenly into the darkness of the castle court. The gate was shut before his eyes and the iron bar dropped into place. He heard Khalil's deep voice at his ear.

"In the name of Allah the Compassionate, let there be an end of madness!"

It was an hour before the Greeks broke down the gate and the mountain peaks were outlined against the first yellow light when they entered the courtyard, weapons in hand.

An hour later the Sebastocrator and the Caesar rode their horses up the ramp that had been cleared of bodies and, surrounded by a strong party of spearmen, searched the palace, the garden and the outbuildings. They were thoroughly mystified by what they found.

A hundred or more Seljuks lay scattered about, dead of sword wounds, and not a horse was in the stables. The palace had been cleared of its treasure, with the exception of the throne of Kai-Kosru, and heavy fretwork and plates of gold. Even the rare silks of Cathay and the ivories of Ethiopia were gone, although the first-comers had rooted out chests of linen and red leather and some weapons — that they hid away immediately.

So Theodore Lascaris, entering the stronghold of Kai-Kosru that noon, found nothing of value awaiting him, and no tidings at all of Sir Hugh. His men reported that they had discovered a light wooden bridge lying at the bottom of the foss that separated the castle from the quarry and, upon further search of the quarry, certain pathways that led into the ravines of the mountain itself.

The only material evidence of Sir Hugh's presence was the steel gauntlet that still lay untouched, by order of the emperor, under the ramp.

Although Theodore had defeated the Turk, had captured Antioch and its castle, his mood was dark that noon, because he had failed to seize the store of the sultan's gold and jewels that was the main object of his crusade. Moreover the Frank was still living, and this did not please the emperor.

True, his men were already creating fables out of the deeds of Sir Hugh, and beginning to believe that the knight of the long sword was a spirit incarnate that roamed the mountains around the Meander during the hours of darkness and disappeared into the bowels of the earth at daybreak.

But to Mavrozomes who was his confidant, Theodore offered a hundred pounds of pure gold and a fief in Nicea for the head of Sir Hugh. And after consultation with his Caesar, he composed a letter to be carried swiftly to Constantinople, before Sir Hugh could journey thither and tell his tale to the main body of crusaders. The letter was addressed to the Count of Flanders.

To the worthy and pious princes of Christendom, greeting: Know that God hath so loved Us that we met the Saracens upon the river Meander, and, though the battle was cruel and hazardous beyond belief, victory was given to Us.

Know also that We have great grief in relating that the Franks under Our command advanced too rashly into the ranks of the Saracens and were sorely beset. Thereupon We gave command to advance Our banner, and did encounter in person the sultan Kai-Kosru, and slay him with Our hand upon the ground after both were unhorsed. Thus did God grant victory to Us, but of the English, the Flemings and French, not a man but was slain.

Know that We intend to set aside a rich portion of the treasure of Antioch, to be paid to the comrades of the slain Franks upon Our return, and this portion will equal the pay of your host for a year.

After a priest had written out this letter and the emperor had signed and sealed it and sent it off by a rider, an order was given to the priest to sprinkle the castle with holy water, and to incense the gauntlet of the Frank that lay before it.

"What say the warriors of my host," he then asked, "concerning this Frank?"

"May it please your Illustriousness," the priest made response earnestly, "they say he is a warlock or werewolf, animate with unholy power, and taking human form in the hours of darkness. Surely he is an agent of Satan."

"Surely," agreed Theodore Lascaris, "though, to my belief, he was slain at the Meander and Satan drew down his body into hell and sent forth a demon in his semblance. Remember that his body was not found at the river."

The priest, breathing deeply, and making the sign of the cross in the air, withdrew. Theodore Lascaris turned to the Caesar who sat at his elbow.

"And now, my Lord Baron, I appoint thee to deal with this fugitive knight. Take a thousand horse, with foot attendants — hie ye straightway to Constantinople, and if this scion of Taranto shows himself in the city, demand audience instantly of his liege lord, the Count of Flanders. Make complaint that Sir Hugh deserted our ranks, allied himself with Saracen Arabs and drew his sword against our men, slaying divers of them, and making off with a great store of gold. But it is also your duty to see that Sir Hugh doth *not* appear at the city."

The Caesar, who was an Italian and could appreciate intrigue, nodded expectantly.

"Send chosen officers," went on the emperor, "to

the seaports, Smyrna, Tenedos and Gallipoli. Have them describe this Frank — his size should be notable, and his hair."

"And the fresh scar on his cheek, sire. I heard it said a spear slashed his face in twain."

"Have him taken and bound and brought secretly to me. Do likewise in the towns of our empire, leaving a band of men to watch in each. Put guards on all the northern caravan routes, and — " he thought for a moment — "fail not to drive off the cattle of the Armenians in these Taurus mountains. Sell the cattle to the Genoese at Smyrna, and from these moneys make a gift to the Count of Flanders, promising him still more."

Having made certain that the roads to the north would be so many traps to catch the knight of Taranto, Theodore Lascaris now awaited the arrival of Mavrozomes, for whom he had sent. Meanwhile he summoned to him two deaf Bulgars, clad in black leather, bearing wolfskins on their shoulders.

When the armorer entered the throne-room of Kai-Kosru and found Theodore seated in the silver chair attended by these twain, Mavrozomes' knees began to quiver and the hair rose on his head.

"Speak," murmured the emperor, eying him.

"May it please your unutterable Grandeur. I found a path through the mountain, cleverly hidden, and at the end — "

"What?"

"Horse tracks."

The emperor smiled.

"So you found horse tracks, but not Sir Hugh?"

Mavrozomes tried to speak and only succeeded in
shaking his head, while his eyes rolled. Whereupon the
emperor made a sign to the two Bulgars, holding out a
slender hand and going through the motions of breaking
off each finger in turn.

Casting himself on the carpet before the dais, the
armorer tried to crawl toward his lord but the two barbarians caught him up in stout arms and haled him
toward the door. To him, thus leaving, Theodore Lascaris addressed a reproof.

"Mavrozomes, I send thee to the rack so thou wilt
taste the pangs shortly to be experienced by Sir Hugh —
until he discloses the hiding place of the sultan's gold. If
Satan bids thee, Mavrozomes, select for him a mock-
emperor of the nether world. Bethink thee and do not
pick out such a one as thou didst for me."

At dawn of the day after, Khalil called in his sentries
and watched the lading of twenty horses with the bags
and goatskins that he had taken from Antioch; he
counted anew the drove of horses brought up by his boys
and found the count a full four hundred — a matter of
pleasure to an Arab, especially as he noticed many

blooded *kohlanis* and Turkoman racers in the stock of
Kai-Kosru.

While the women bundled up the woolen tents and
his warriors saddled the steeds they had selected for the
day's journey from the camp on the mountain, Khalil
strode off in an amiable mood to talk to his two captive
Franks.

He was still mystified, and he proposed to be
enlightened. At the time they rode from the castle of
Antioch, Khalil had been certain that Sir Hugh was
ahmak, mad. Now that the crusader had quieted down
and his wounds had been dressed, Khalil was not so sure
he was mad.

Entering the tent where the captives sat, he squatted
down on the rug by Sir Hugh and looked at him reflectively. Being a chieftain, he greeted the knight
courteously, and being a Moslem spoke of something
that had no bearing on his visit.

"Eh, Donn Dera, I see that thy companion has the
long sword that wrought such woe among the Roumis."

The man from Erin nodded moodily.

"Yes, Khalil, my joints are stiff. Since I can not deal
a blow with the great sword Durandal, I have given it to
Sir Hugh. Faith. I am thinking that no other man could
handle it."

"All things are possible with Allah," murmured the
Arab. He glanced at the sword that the young knight was

wiping down with a soft cloth until the steel shone as with an inward fire. So, too, the dark eyes of Khalil glowed. Every detail of the fight at the ramp was fixed in his memory.

Sir Hugh kept silence, fearing that the Arabs would try to take the sword from him, now that their truce was at an end.

"Eh," said Khalil again. "From the gate I beheld the emperor of the Greeks with his standard. Now it is clear to me that this lord is not the emperor."

And he glanced sharply at Donn Dera.

"True," assented that warrior promptly. "It befell in this wise, O Khalil. The Greeks selected a false emperor at the Meander to draw the attack of their foes. They appareled him in all things like the real Commenus, and this man was Sir Hugh."

"Mash'allah!" Khalil thought this over for a while. "Who may escape his fate?"

"I have told thee truth," Sir Hugh spoke for the first time, bluntly. "I am the knight of Taranto, the vassal of a Frankish count, who will ransom us twain from Constantinople if thou wilt send thither."

"Will the antelope go into the tiger's lair?" Khalil shook his head, good-naturedly. "Thyself lacks wisdom, Lord, to offer thus."

"Yea," quoth Donn Dera grimly. "He will never be a king. He lacks wisdom and there is no help for it.

Throughout his life he will be set upon and tricked, and he will suffer for others' wrongs. When that is said, the worst is said.

"Reckless he is, and stubborn, and death lies in wait for those who follow him. Yet in the courts of the kings of all the world there is no champion the like of him — who held the gate of Antioch against eight thousand men and drove them back. Yea, he threw down his glove and bade the men of weapons come against it. It is an honor to me that I shall have the telling of this thing to the end of my life. For ye can not say better of any man that *that*."

The faded eyes of the wanderer gleamed reminiscently.

And so I have given him the great sword that was found by my cunning, to keep."

When Khalil had considered this, two things were clear to him. He would have chosen to keep Sir Hugh with him as companion in his wars — and in honor, according to the code of a chieftain of the elder Ibna, he could not ransom or sell as a slave a man who had fought at his side.

"May Allah grant ye an open road!"

He rose, gathering his cloak about him.

"The agreement is at an end. Thou art free to choose thine own path. Two good horses with saddle bags are my gifts."

"The gift of a prince," cried the man from Erin. "We

will e'en fare to Smyrna and go by the coast to Constantinople to complain of this dog-emperor."

"Not so!" said the knight.

"Where else?"

Sir Hugh stood up, supporting himself on the cross
piece of Durandal.

"Long years ago, I made a pledge to God, and this I
must redeem. When I took the Cross I made a vow to
seek the sepulcher of Christ, and not to turn back from
this venture. I have thrown down the gage to Theodore
Lascaris and with him will I deal in another day. Now,
Khalil fares to the south, through Palestine. Surely he
will grant us his escort to Jerusalem!"

Khalil uttered an exclamation of pleasure, for Sir
Hugh had invoked a thing cherished by him, his hospi-
tality.

"Come then, as my guest, and surely my honor is
increased thereby."

He glanced inquiringly at Donn Dera.

"Hard to say," quoth the wanderer. "Yea, I will
come, to shield this youth with my cunning, for I love
him."

Picking up his bundle and his flail, Donn Dera
went from the tent and peered around for his horse,
while Khalil swaggered off calling to his men.

"O ye sons of Yaman, Allah hath caused great profit
to us this day, for the wonder-working sword goes with

us to Jerusalem, and the Frank who is undoubtedly mad, but only in certain things, after the manner of his kind. Bring the horses!"

And so swiftly did the tribe melt from the passes of the Taurus that the outriders of the Caesar who were looking for cattle saw only their dust drifting into the desert plain, and the gleam of the sword that was as long as a spear, and that was thereafter the cause of sorrow to Theodore Lascaris.

But, being wiser than Mavrozomes, the Caesar said naught of this to the emperor.